PLAYING WITH FIRE

D0608737

Jonathan Harlen

A & C Black • London

First published in the UK in 2009 by
A & C Black Publishers Ltd
36 Soho Square, London, W1D 3QY

www.acblack.com

First published in Australia as *Blood Sports* by
Scholastic Press
An imprint of Scholastic Australia Pty Limited

Text copyright © 2008 Jonathan Harlen

The right of Jonathan Harlen to be identified
as the author of this work has been asserted by
him in accordance with the Copyrights,
Designs and Patents Act 1988.

ISBN 978-1-4081-1359-2

This book is produced using paper that is made from
wood grown in managed, sustainable forests. It is natural,
renewable and recyclable. The logging and manufacturing
processes conform to the environmental regulations of
the country of origin.

Printed and bound in Great Britain
by CPI Cox & Wyman, Reading, RG1 8EX.

1. THE KIDNAPPING

We had just walked past the halfway line when we heard it.

The heavy, thudding sound of a helicopter, coming in low over the hills.

The sound very quickly got louder. Choppers aren't known for their lightning speed, but this baby was certainly moving. It was flying without lights as well. By the time we picked out its shape silhouetted against the night sky above the floodlights, it was right on top of us.

It swooped in and landed in a corner of the training field, 40 metres away.

As soon as it touched down, a side door opened. Six men hit the ground running. They were wearing balaclavas, and were dressed in black combat fatigues. All six of them were carrying assault rifles. Without a word, they fanned out and sprinted across the field towards us.

It was nine o'clock in the evening. There were only three people on the training field: me, Frank the Turk, and the recently appointed coach of the Wallabies, Kelvin Hunt. Frank and I were in camp with the Wallabies in Coffs Harbour, watching Hunt try to rebuild the team after Australia's miserable failure in the World Cup. As head of the boxing programme at the Australian Institute of Sport and a former professional super-heavyweight boxer, Frank was doing some conditioning work with the players. He had been hired to improve their punching combinations, so they could brawl better in South African nightclubs. Their performance in this area had been sadly lacklustre in recent years.

As for me, I had nothing better to do, so I was tagging along for the ride. A weekend with Frank at a Coffs Harbour resort, watching the Wallabies go through their paces, had sounded like pretty good fun to me.

Now suddenly it wasn't fun at all. We were under attack. We were blocked off from the resort, caught right out in the open, with no time to escape. There was no way we could outrun those guns.

'Get down!' Frank yelled. He and I dropped, stomach-first, onto the spongy green turf of the playing field. Kelvin Hunt, however, was a man used to giving orders, not taking them. He stayed on his feet, rooted to the spot. He blinked at the approaching commandos like a deer caught in the headlights.

Hang on a minute, his expression seemed to say. *Did I book a helicopter and a SWAT team in balaclavas for nine o'clock? What's going on?*

The team leader made a silent signal to the others. They swarmed in around Hunt, ignoring Frank and me completely.

Hunt backed away, shouting at the top of his voice, as four men grabbed him and pinned his arms. Hunt kept struggling. He kicked out with his legs. He bucked and wriggled. He even managed to hit the team leader with a nice Glasgow kiss. The team leader didn't like that too much. He stepped in and clocked Hunt on the side of the head with the butt of his assault rifle.

Hunt stayed upright, but his head was lolling. He was out for the count. Six pairs of hands clutched at his sagging body. The commandos dragged him quickly and expertly back to the chopper, and shoved him inside the open door. They leapt in nimbly beside him, drew the door shut, and then – barely a minute after they had landed – they took off again, arcing up and over the training ground, above the blazing floodlights, and made a beeline back towards the hills.

2. The Kelvinator

Kelvin 'the Kelvinator' Hunt was a controversial figure. He was a hard man who'd packed down in the second row back in his playing days with Sydney Uni. He didn't score too many tries, or make too many busting runs up the middle of the pack, but if you wanted an ear bitten off, or an eye gouged out, or an opposition fly-half quietly rendered unconscious in the contact area, he was your man. Rumour had it that he collected the ears he bit off and the eyes he gouged out. He took them home, dipped them in milk and egg yolk, then fried them up for breakfast, sprinkled with seasoning and breadcrumbs.

Hunt had been appointed to toughen up

the Australian scrum, which had been steamrollered by the English and the South Africans. He'd been hammering forward play all week. Three full-on, two-hour training sessions per day. The scrum, Hunt said, was the heart and soul of rugby union. It was power. It was passion. It was one man pushing two men up three men's bums. The forwards had spent long hours learning the finer points of his no-nonsense approach. They had hurled themselves at the scrum machines so many times that when they went out for a surf in the morning they instinctively packed down to throw themselves into a wave.

Hunt didn't believe in mollycoddling. He didn't give two hoots about his players' egos, their reputations, or their fragile self-esteem. The closest he got to praise was letting loose with a torrent of slightly less filthy abuse. 'Garbage! Pathetic! That was hopeless, you skirts!' meant he was delighted with the players' efforts. So did 'Come on, you pack of pansies! Muscle up! I've had cups of Starbucks coffee stronger than that!'

The players had been training hard for five days by the time Frank and I arrived. They didn't have a lot left. In fact, I'd seen walruses in a sauna with more spring in their step. I'd seen better blind-side combinations from month-old roadkill. But strangely, not a single one of the players protested. No one spat the dummy. No one gave Hunt an earful and stomped off home, saying, 'Stuff this, I'm going back to my old job reconditioning fridges.'

The first night we were there, Hunt sent them off on a scrum run. He made them all pack down in scrums and stay in formation. Then he sent them out of the resort, up the hill to the main road, and north 12 miles to Woolgoolga.

'Ten laps round the Sikh temple, 500 push-ups, then back here again!' he'd shouted at them. 'Come on then, get moving! What are youse waitin' for? Go!'

The two assistant coaches had headed off with the players. It was the first time Frank and I had been alone with Hunt. He stood with his arms folded, watching until the players had disappeared up the road, chuckling to himself. He turned to face us with a lopsided grin.

'So, what d'y'reckon, boys?' he said. 'That oughta sort out the spiders from the cockroaches, eh?'

'You're working them pretty hard, Kel,' I said.

Hunt slapped a fatherly hand on my shoulder. 'Kid,' he said, 'I don't know how much you know about sport, but it's five per cent talent, 40 per cent skill, and 99.9 per cent blood and guts. You got that?'

'Wow,' I said. 'That's 144.9 per cent.'

'If you don't put the effort in, you don't win,' Hunt said. 'And when you don't win, you lose. Is that simple enough for you?'

'Sure,' I said. 'Unless you draw.'

'We've just come off a losing streak longer

then the Amazon river,' Hunt went on. 'We lost to *Romania*, for Pete's sake! We drew with the Canary Islands! We gotta get back to basics. Like I said to the head of the Federation when he asked me what areas I thought the national team could improve on. "What areas?" I said. "What *areas*? How about that great big green one, out there?"'

He roared with laughter at this, slapping me so hard I nearly fell over.

'I told the Federation straight-up,' he went on. '"To get Australia back on track, you need the best coach in the world. The absolute top guy. Bar none." So they said, "Kelvin, do you truly believe you're the best in the world?" And I said, "Maybe. Maybe not. But I'm definitely in the top one."'

He roared with laughter and slapped me a second time. You had to like the guy, even though he had a voice louder than David Beckham's tattoos and an ego the size of Kevin Pietersen's lunch. He looked the part, too, with his squashed nose, square chin, missing teeth and wiry mass of leonine grey-blond hair. He looked like the Wild Man of Borneo after a week of electric-shock therapy. No wonder the press and the Federation loved him. No wonder people all over the country were hailing him as the next saviour of Australian rugby. Whatever the 'it' factor is in coaching, he had it in spades.

And now he'd been kidnapped.

3. FLINTOFF ON THE CASE

Frank and I were the only ones who had seen the commandos up close. We couldn't tell the police much, though. The helicopter was black. The commandos were black. They were in black balaclavas and black combat fatigues, carrying black assault rifles. No one had looked at us, or spoken a single word during the whole operation. It had been very professionally done.

The police conducted interviews at the resort all night. The following morning, Hunt was still missing. Word got out to the press, and the manure hit the extraction equipment well and truly.

The head of the Australian Rugby Federation issued a press statement condemning 'this cowardly act of sporting terrorism' and stating that it 'will not stop our great rugby-loving nation from marching to victory in the next World Cup'.

Shortly afterwards, the New Zealand Rugby Federation issued a brief statement condemning the act and denying any responsibility. The South African Federation also quickly denied any involvement. So did the English. The Italians and Argentineans sent their best wishes to the players and to Hunt's family. The Japanese sent their best wishes, as well as two small, tastefully wrapped gift boxes of traditional Hokkaido shortbread. The Irish, the Scots and the Welsh gave three cheers and headed to the pub. The Romanians only heard about the whole thing six months later, when the mail arrived in Bucharest by mule.

As for the French, news of the kidnapping threw them into a profound existential crisis. In cafés across the nation's capital, stylish, Gauloises-smoking Parisians pondered the underlying philosophical issues.

'What does this mean?' mused Professor Antoine Le Flouffe of the Sorbonne. 'Is it *really* a kidnapping? Or is it, in fact, society that has been kidnapped? Who are the *real* victims here?'

Next morning at breakfast, Frank and I sat with the Wallabies squad and Hunt's two assistant coaches in the resort dining room. We had been up all night. No news on Hunt had filtered back to us. As the players ploughed through their ten-stacks of pancakes with maple syrup, the conversation naturally turned to who they believed was responsible.

'It's the South Africans,' one of the front-row forwards said emphatically. 'Those Boers. They haven't forgiven us for the thrashing we gave them in 2006.'

'Nah, it's the Kiwis for sure,' the reserve half-back piped up. 'They know we're as good as them now. They're trembling in their boots.'

'What are you talking about?' said one of the wingers. 'They flogged us last time.'

'Yeah,' someone echoed. 'And the time before that.'

'Look, we're *improving*, that's all I'm saying,' the half-back said. 'And it's all down to the Kelvinator, right? Without him, we'd still be losing to Romania. We'd still be drawing with the Canary Islands. So the Kiwis reckon, why not kidnap him, and keep him holed up in a cave in the Southern Alps until the next World Cup is over? That way they *know* they're going to win.'

There was a brooding silence. Talking about the All Blacks always made the mood in the Wallabies camp a little grim.

'Shame about their wives and girlfriends, though,' someone else said.

'Eh?' said the half-back.

'New rule for the next World Cup. They've been banned from the games, 'cause they keep jumping the fence and eating the grass.'

By lunchtime we were still all milling around the resort. Now, don't get me wrong – milling around in a five-star luxury resort in Coffs Harbour with 30-odd international rugby players is not such a terrible thing. But the Wallabies had come to train, not lounge by the pool in designer swimsuits, sipping cocktails. They'd run out of sheep jokes. The police wouldn't let them use the scrum machines. There were only so many ten-stacks of pancakes with maple syrup they could eat.

I had a suspicion the case would prove too big for the local police. So I was not a bit surprised when, at one o'clock, a posse of suited-and-sunglassed heavies from the Federal Sports Crime Unit in Canberra breezed in, fresh from the airport. Nor was I shocked to see that they were led by my old mate Detective Inspector Flintoff.

Flintoff was a thick-necked, pear-shaped copper in his mid-50s. Like a lot of coppers, he loved his sport. He'd been on the books with the South Sydney Rabbitohs in his early 20s, my father once told me, and had cut quite a dashing figure. Nowadays the only thing he cut was the blood supply to his brain every time he broke a sweat. He didn't dash anywhere. He waddled. If the marine rescue squad at Sea World happened to see him in swimming trunks lying on a beach, they'd tow him back out to the ocean.

I was coming back from the toilet when he walked into the dining room. I was the very first person he saw, which I'm sure did not improve his blood pressure one bit. He stopped in his tracks, dead in front of me. His face turned heart-attack purple.

'Fletcher Smith!' he snapped. 'What are *you* doing here, kid? Shouldn't you be up at the nursing home with your old man?'

'It's not a nursing home,' I said. 'It's a health farm. And it's in Switzerland. Which is a little out of my way.'

'The sooner you're out of everybody's

way, the better,' Flintoff growled. 'Don't think you're going to be doing any work on *this* case, kid. This is a matter of national security.'

He glared at me, massaging the tip of his bristly moustache with his bottom lip. 'So how is your old man, anyway?' he said, a little lamely. 'Is he improving?'

Now I *was* surprised. This was the first time Flintoff had ever expressed concern for my father. The two of them had been bitter rivals for 20 years. Flintoff had done everything he could to get my father kicked out of the police force. In the end, my father hadn't waited around to be fired. He'd quit the Sports Crime Unit to become a private eye, working the same beat.

A lot of their disagreements had been about Samson Bolivar, the billionaire Gold Coast-based sports management guru, who later arranged the car crash that crippled my parents. My father had been chasing Bolivar for years. Flintoff thought Bolivar was squeaky clean.

'He's no better, no worse,' I said. 'Same with Mum. They've got some kind of post-traumatic amnesia. They recognise each other. They recognise Frank and me. But that's about it.'

'Tough, kid,' Flintoff said. 'I feel for you. But if you still think you're gonna be a sports detective like your old man, you need to be in that nut farm along with him.'

'I'm here with Frank,' I said. 'He was hired to do some conditioning. I'm not on the case.'

'Good,' Flintoff said. 'But you still need to make a statement. Everybody does. Lieutenant Calabria here will take the details.'

Every time I saw Flintoff he had a new assistant. He went through them like a kitchen maid goes through dishcloths. Last time I'd crossed paths with him, he'd had an eager beaver named Jinks as his attack dog. This time it was a chick – I mean a young woman. She had olive skin and jet-black hair, which she wore fiercely short. Her uniform was trim and neat, and the expression in her steely brown eyes told me she would perhaps not appreciate my extensive repertoire of Italian football World Cup jokes.

'Hi,' I said.

'Sit down, Mr Smith.'

'Are you going to make me an offer I can't refuse?' I asked hopefully.

'No, I'm just going to ask you a few questions. It won't take long.'

We sat at one of the spare dining tables. There were three restaurants attached to the lobby of the resort. One for breakfast, one for lunch, one for dinner. There was another (much more expensive) restaurant out on an island in the middle of the resort lake. To get to this restaurant, you had to tie several stacks of hundred-dollar bills together into a raft, paddle out with your cheque-book stubs, lighting up the water with the glow of your burning credit cards.

Then, when you arrived, you handed your wallet to the chef and he fed it to a shark.

Lieutenant Calabria pulled out a PDA. You know the one, I'm sure. Mobile phone. Personal organiser. Email. Permanent Internet. Direct hotline to ASIO, MI5, the CIA, Mossad and the FBI. *Much* more upmarket than a paper and pen.

'Name?' she said.

'Fletcher Smith.'

'Address?'

'Australian Institute of Sport, Canberra.'

She blinked at me in puzzlement. 'You're an athlete?' she asked.

'Absolutely. Can't you tell?'

'You look a little . . . young.'

'Yeah, that's the special diet I'm on. It's a mixture of creatine, massive-weight-gain powder, grated cheese and horse tranquilliser. It makes me age backwards.'

'How old are you, Fletcher?'

'Fourteen.'

'You're not on a scholarship, are you?'

'No,' I admitted. 'But I do live at the Institute. In the Sports Commission building. And I *am* an athlete. You want to see me sprint across the lobby?'

'Just tell me what you know about the kidnapping.' Those steely brown eyes were killing me. 'That way I *might* get to interview someone else before midnight.'

There wasn't much to tell. I tried to spin it out as long as possible. Talking to the lovely Lieutenant Calabria made a nice change from watching the Wallabies' front row stick their heads up each other's bums. I identified the helicopter as a Eurocopter Panther, although I wasn't 100 per cent sure about that, given that it was dark and there'd been a fair amount of glare from the floodlights. But I was *pretty* sure.

'That's not usually an army helicopter,' I told her. 'They're used for rescue work in this country, so it was probably surplus. I'd say it fell off the back of a truck, if you know what I mean.'

'You think it was stolen?' Lieutenant Calabria punched some keys on her PDA. 'Or do you think it was the Army who did the kidnapping?'

'Hard to tell,' I said. 'Everything was black. Even the kidnappers. They could be rogue Army, but I'm guessing it's a classic indie bad-guy operation. The only thing missing was the Dr Evil logo.'

'A Eurocopter Panther,' Lieutenant Calabria repeated. 'Thank you. We'll follow that up.'

'And the assault rifles were M-16s,' I said. 'They'll be stolen, too. There'll be a network for them in this country. Gunrunners trade them all the time. There won't be any sort of network for the chopper, because it's a one-off. Someone will have made sure the trail has gone cold. But I'm willing to bet that the same supplier provided both.'

Lieutenant Calabria kept tapping away at her PDA. 'Why do you say that?' she asked.

'Because there aren't many arms dealers you can trust,' I replied. 'Once you find one, you tend to stick with them.'

She paused, looking up at me doubtfully. 'Fletcher,' she said, 'Just what exactly do you do at the Institute?'

'I do my father's job,' I replied. 'He was Director of Sports Forensics at the AIS. Ex-cop turned sports private eye. Used to work with your boss, Flintoff. Until Flintoff fired him. Last year he got hurt in a car crash arranged by Samson Bolivar.'

The lovely lieutenant's eyebrow flickered. Was it possible that Flintoff had already mentioned Bolivar to her, and to the rest of his team? If he had, it was probably just to absolutely, categorically deny that Bolivar was a suspect. On the other hand, maybe Bolivar was linked to the kidnapping somehow. Maybe some kind of shady business deal was involved. Shady business deals followed Bolivar like ducklings followed mother duck.

I decided it might be worth a little private, unpaid sports sleuthing to find out.

4. THE LAPTOP

After lunch, Frank and I returned to the training pitch. There was one last thing I wanted to check out before we left. The day Kelvin Hunt disappeared had been overcast and rainy. The pitch had taken several heavy showers earlier that afternoon. It was soft and spongy, much more spongy than normal – a fact I couldn't help noticing when I'd thrown myself onto it, face-first.

I wanted to see if any of Dr Evil's henchmen had left footprints.

We found the spot where the chopper had landed, and searched from there. No one else was with us. Some of Flintoff's SCU posse were still down at the resort, interviewing staff and guests. Flintoff himself had headed west, to supervise the search for the helicopter up in the hills behind Coffs Harbour. Training had been cancelled for the day while the Rugby Union Federation met to decide what to do with the team.

We did find some prints. They were right on the spot where the kidnappers had jumped out of the chopper. They'd landed with such force that the close-cut grass had been pressed down and stamped – literally – into the dirt. There were two clean sets of bootprints, each from about a size eleven boot, and shaped like this:

It wasn't an army boot. I knew that much. A set of prints from standard army boots looks more like this:

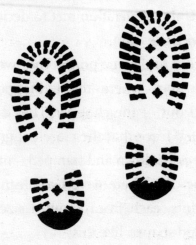

This was something completely different. But what?

'Who wears a tread like that on their boots?' I asked Frank after we had both inspected the prints carefully and agreed we didn't have a clue. 'Basketballers?'

'Oh, sure,' Frank said. 'That makes sense. The West Sydney Razorbacks have kidnapped Hunt, so he can work on their free throws.'

'Whoever they are, they're all wearing exactly the same shoes,' I said. 'It's some kind of uniform. No doubt about that.'

'The next thing we've got to sort out,' I said to Frank as we packed our bags back in our hotel room, 'is who might have a motive for the kidnapping. Apart from the other rugby federations, that is. And I really don't think they're involved.'

'There is someone who might have a personal motive,' Frank suggested. 'What about Lachlan Maddox? Didn't Hunt dump him as captain, right after he got appointed? Told him to pack his bags and leave.'

I nodded. Lachlan Maddox, the former captain of the Wallabies for six years, would certainly have a motive. Thanks to Hunt, his career was now in ruins. He'd been so devastated at being stripped of the captaincy, he'd quit the game.

'And let's not forget the coach Hunt replaced,' I added. 'Tim Jamieson. He refused to quit even after the failure in the World Cup. So they had to fire him. Could be sour grapes there.'

'Then there's Hunt's wife,' Frank went on. 'Or maybe a mistress. Some kind of love triangle? You can never rule them out.'

'All right, but why a *kidnapping*?' I said. 'Why a helicopter? In the middle of a training session? At Coffs Harbour? Why not just hire a hit man to pop him one when he steps out of his front door?'

'Kidnappings usually mean a ransom,' Frank replied. 'Maybe it's purely a money-making exercise. Could be that no one he knows was involved at all.'

That one hadn't occurred to me. But it was definitely another possibility. All it took was a group of professionals – mercenaries, maybe ex-Army, there were plenty of them around – who knew the value of someone like Hunt. So they snatch him, hole up somewhere in the bush for a month or so, then hit the Federation for a cool ten million and wait till somebody pays.

'I'm thinking maybe Hunt's family's the target,' Frank went on. 'That's the way it works with football players in South America. There are a couple of high-profile cases every year. The families pay up; the footballers get returned safe and sound. It's almost an honest line of business in that part of the world.'

'Whoever they are, they had help on the inside,' I said. 'They knew everything about that training session last night. They knew exactly what time Hunt would finish. They knew he always hangs around after his sessions, to personally clean up. They knew *exactly what time* he would be out there on his own. They knew what field he would be training on. Someone had to tell them those things.'

'Maybe they had access to his laptop,' Frank said. 'His session plans are all stored on his computer. Every single one of them. I've seen them.'

I stopped packing. I stared at him. Sometimes Frank could be more than just a pretty face. 'The laptop!' I breathed. 'Of course! That's brilliant! What room was Hunt in? Maybe the laptop's still there.'

'Whoa, now!' Frank laughed. 'This isn't our case, champ. No one's paying us, remember? No pay, no play.'

'Bolivar might be involved,' I said. 'When I was making my statement, I got a strong feeling that he was. If we could get any evidence to link him to this kidnapping, he'd go away for life. That's the least he deserves, after what he did to my parents.'

'Fletcher, there's nothing linking this to him,' Frank said patiently. 'Nothing at all.'

'No, but it's right up his street, isn't it? Kidnapping the Wallabies' coach? Who else but Bolivar would dream up something like that? And if someone *did* download those training sessions, there'll be a record of it on the hard drive. I just want to check, that's all. If there's no link to Bolivar, I'll let it go.'

5. Smash and Grab

Hunt's 'room' turned out to be the most expensive private bungalow in the entire place. It was set in half an acre of tropical gardens, down a path away from the rest of the resort, surrounded on three sides by a two-metre-high brush fence. It had its own swimming pool and barbecue area, as well as spectacular views of the ocean. Nothing but the best for the next saviour of Australian rugby.

No police were visible from the outside. I got Frank to give me a leg-up, then climbed over the fence. Dropping down quietly on the other side, I approached the back door through the gardens. I kept tight to the wall, and peered through the partly drawn curtains to the living room.

Hunt's laptop was right there on the table. That was the good news. The bad news was that Lieutenant Calabria was seated at the table with her back to me, scrolling through a file.

'So *she's* the computer whiz,' I muttered to myself. 'Yeah, that figures.'

I explained our problem to Frank when I'd got back over the fence. 'You still want to try and get the laptop?' Frank asked.

'No,' I said. 'You're the heavy. You get it.'

Frank only laughed. He's always been a disappointment as a heavy, to tell you the truth. He's not the deranged, fiendishly cruel, bloodthirsty Turkish killbot that I hoped he would be. Since his retirement from professional boxing (he lost his super-heavyweight WWF world title to a giant panda at Madison Square Garden) he has rarely used his wonderful natural-born talent for extreme violence. Sometimes he's so downright mushy and woolly headed,

I think he's a closet social worker. He needs to quit his job as head of the boxing programme at the Institute and become a priest.

'So here's the plan,' I went on. 'We hit the bungalow in broad daylight, relying completely on the element of surprise. You kick the door down and bust into the living room, firing your Beretta in the air and swearing in Turkish. The lieutenant screams in terror and drops to the floor. You grab the laptop, karate-chop the table in half, then smash your way out through the nearest window. If the lieutenant moves, shoot her in the knee.'

'No,' Frank said.

I could only shake my head. Honestly. What a killjoy. Good heavies are just so hard to find these days.

As I expected, it was all down to me. That laptop could be the key to nailing Bolivar. It was only a hunch, but it was a chance I had to take. I scanned the top of the fence surrounding the bungalow, searching for a viable Plan B.

To our right was a small gate where a path led through the fence to the front door of the bungalow. Two small stone statues of Buddha stood at the sides of the path.

'Could you lift one of them?' I asked Frank.

He frowned. 'Maybe. Why?'

'Could you *throw* it? Over the fence and into the pool?'

I explained my new idea. Frank was deeply impressed. He was so deeply impressed, in fact, that he refused to have anything to do with it, because he didn't want to dilute its genius.

'Fletcher, you have gone beyond desperate,' he said. 'You are now officially being pathetic. It'll never work.'

'It's my only chance!' I said. 'Once she's finished with the laptop she'll take it away as evidence. We'll never see it again!'

'You'll get yourself arrested. You can't

possibly steal that laptop when she is seated right in front of it.'

'Frank, I've calculated the odds. The probability of capture and arrest is 23.16 per cent. Trust me.'

The roof of Hunt's bungalow featured several state-of-the-art self-opening skylights, to let in natural light. Frank and I could see a couple of these skylights from the path. One had been opened up like a sunroof on a sports car, to assist with interior air flow and reduce the need for air-conditioning. All part of being eco-friendly, don't you know.

My plan was to go in through the skylight. Frank would chuck the Buddha into the pool, where it would hopefully make a fairly loud splash. The lovely Lieutenant Calabria would leave the bungalow, and come out into the back garden to see what had landed in the water. At that point I would drop down through the skylight, onto the sofa positioned (from memory) directly below it. I would grab the laptop and be out the front door before Lieutenant Calabria returned.

No sweat. As I said to Frank: probability of capture and arrest, 23.16 per cent.

Five minutes later, I was up on the roof. Getting to the skylight wasn't easy. The roof was steep, and also uncomfortably hot, with the mid-afternoon January sun beating down on it. I had initially thought I could climb up in bare feet, to try to keep noise to a minimum, but the tiles on the roof were far too hot for that.

I climbed very slowly to avoid making any noise. Mostly, I slid upwards on my stomach. By the time I reached the skylight, the heat radiating up through my body was intense. I was starting to feel well and truly char-grilled.

Maybe my brain got a little overheated. That might explain what happened next. It certainly wasn't Frank's fault – he hurled that Buddha statue over the fence and into the swimming pool like a seasoned pro.

As I'd hoped, it made an almighty splash. Looking down through the skylight, I saw Lieutenant Calabria get up, puzzled. She left the laptop on the table in the living room, and made her way quickly out through the sliding door into the back garden.

That was my cue. I wriggled between the skylight and the roof and prepared to drop down. It was the dropping part that got me into trouble. I landed on the sofa all right, but unfortunately for me it wasn't a regular sofa – it was a sofa *bed*. Hidden underneath the cushions was a minefield of metal supports, springs, bars, hinges and levers. I landed right at the line on the back of the sofa where the horizontal cushions met the vertical. I was dropping with such force that I kept on going. All the way through.

Instead of bouncing off, I was swallowed up by the sofa bed. My legs disappeared up over my knees. The mangled metal underneath scraped six inches of skin off my shins. When I tried to move I sank deeper into the bowels of the wretched thing and felt the metal innards scrape against my shins even more.

I was trapped.

I was in pain.

I bellowed. I yelped. I howled.

I was still howling when Lieutenant Calabria came in from checking out the Buddha in the swimming pool. If she was surprised by the Buddha, she was even more surprised to see me getting eaten by the sofa bed.

'Fletcher! What the –? How did you get in here?'

I couldn't talk. The pain was too much. I pointed up towards the skylight.

'You jumped down from the *roof*?'

'I'm stuck!' I gasped. 'It's killing me! It's eating me alive! Get me out!'

Lieutenant Calabria pulled the cushions off the sofa bed. She found a bar somewhere that opened it, and gave that a yank. The tangle of metal around my legs creaked and twanged, loosening just enough for me to lift myself free.

'Owwwwww!' I said. 'I'm bleeding! Owww! Owww!'

'Fletcher, this is a restricted area.' The lieutenant sounded shocked. 'You can't come in here. You know that. What was that thing you threw into the pool?'

'It's a Buddha!' I said. 'Owwwwww! Hurt! Hurt!'

I climbed out of the bed onto the carpet. My shins were a terrible sight. They looked like they had been attacked by a school of piranhas. I walked gingerly around the table with the laptop on it, trying to lessen the pain. It didn't work.

'You jumped in through the roof?' Lieutenant Calabria repeated. 'I don't know whether to arrest you, or . . . call a psychiatrist. What is going on?'

'Do you have a bandage or something?' I said. 'Please? I'm bleeding.'

'I . . . um . . . there might be something

in the bathroom,' Lieutenant Calabria said. 'Stay there. I'll check.'

Sometimes there are advantages to being 14. If Frank had tried the same drop-down-through-the-skylight routine on a federal police officer investigating a kidnapping, he would've ended up spending a month behind bars. But for me, it was different. I was just a kid. Lieutenant Calabria wandered off into the bathroom to find me some bandages.

Leaving the laptop right there on the table.

Stealing it was out of the question. I could hardly walk, so my getaway with the laptop tucked under my arm would be a little slow. Second, Lieutenant Calabria already knew who I was. This severely limited my chances of melting away into the shadows undetected. But maybe there was another way to get what I wanted. A trick I remembered from days long ago, back in high school.

Copying.

I delved in my pocket for my memory stick. I'd brought it along with me in case I had to get information from the laptop fast. I slotted it into a USB port and began copying Hunt's itinerary, diary and training schedule, as well as the computer's security log.

To buy time while this command was processing I hobbled down the hallway towards the bathroom.

'Got anything?' I asked.

'There's some bandages here,' Lieutenant Calabria said. 'Come in.'

I hobbled into the bathroom. I raised my foot up on the rim of the bathtub and Lieutenant Calabria began dressing and bandaging one of my shins.

'Now tell me,' she said. 'Be honest. What are you doing here?'

I took a deep breath. 'I need to check that laptop,' I said. 'It's for my own investigation. I'm trying to get some dirt on Bolivar. It's for my dad.'

I explained in more detail how I believed Bolivar had caused the crash that had injured my parents. I also explained why I thought Bolivar might be involved in the kidnapping of Kelvin Hunt. Of course, it was the good lieutenant's own tiny flicker of the eyebrow that had suggested this to me in the first place. Now I got a chance to study her reaction again. Judging by the length of her pause and the difficulty she had in finding the right thing to say to me, my initial hunch had been correct. There was more than a slim chance Bolivar was involved.

'Look, I know you can't talk about it,' I said. 'And I know I'm just a kid. But my father had lots of connections. I've got some as well. Frank and I could find out stuff in one week that you guys couldn't learn in ten years.'

Lieutenant Calabria smiled. 'Like what?' she said.

'Like Bolivar's movements. I mean *all* of them. Everyone he meets. Everywhere he goes. Anyone on his payroll, official or otherwise. If he *is* linked to this kidnapping in some way, you need to do some digging. I can dig better than anybody.'

Her smile changed to a frown. 'How?'

'I have my sources,' I said. 'I can't say any more than that.'

'Interesting.' The lieutenant rolled the second bandage around the calf of my left leg. 'I wonder why the DI never mentioned you. Or your father. Does he know anything about these . . . sources?'

'Flintoff?' I snorted. 'Are you kidding? First, I would never tell him anything. I wouldn't trust him an inch. And second, he thinks I'm a pest. We have a mutual non-admiration society. As you can see.'

'He's a decent copper, Fletcher.'

'No, he's not. He's a blind fool. If it wasn't for him, my parents would never have been injured. And Bolivar would be behind bars.'

Lieutenant Calabria finished bandaging.

Both my shins were now smothered in Savlon and swaddled in coils of clean linen. They looked ridiculous, but they felt a whole lot better.

Lieutenant Calabria tidied up. She and I walked back out into the living room. Kelvin Hunt's laptop was still there on the table, exactly where the lieutenant had left it. My memory stick was still there, too, quietly working away. A quick glance at the screen told me that the command I had entered had been executed.

'You wouldn't let me borrow that laptop for a while, would you?' I said.

'I can't do that, Fletcher. You know I can't.'

'No worries.' I grinned at her. 'I don't need to borrow it now anyway.'

I reached out and removed the memory stick from the back of the laptop. As Lieutenant Calabria's eyes widened, I capped it and dropped it in my back pocket.

'You didn't see that,' I said. 'It never existed. And if anyone asks, I was never here.'

6. HOLDEN McGROYNE

The search for Kelvin Hunt intensified over the next week. Every so often, Flintoff appeared on TV to give the eager public another update on how rapidly things were not progressing.

'We haven't found him yet,' 'We *still* haven't found him,' 'We're looking, but not in any of the right places.' At least, that's what Flintoff *should* have said. But Flintoff was a master at conducting long-winded press conferences without actually saying anything at all.

The Federal Sports Crime Unit concentrated their search in the mountainous bush country west of Coffs Harbour. Many people – including Frank and me – had heard the helicopter fly off in that direction. We assumed that the kidnappers had returned to a hide-out somewhere in that area, or maybe further west, and were keeping Hunt nice and safe until they were ready to issue their demands.

In the media, all sorts of feverish speculation began to take hold. The most popular theory, at least in Sydney, was that Hunt had actually kidnapped himself, in a cynical publicity stunt designed to rally support and bring back the fans after the Wallabies' failure at the World Cup.

This theory was the brainchild of the chief sports reporter for the *Sydney Daily Herald*, Holden McGroyne. McGroyne was a former Balmain rugby-league legend who had waged a one-man war on rugby union for years. In his column for the weekend edition of the *Daily Herald*, *Holden McGroyne On Sunday Morning*, he wrote:

ARE THERE NO DEPTHS TO WHICH THESE SHAMELESS SELF-PROMOTING RUGBY UNION LUNATICS WILL NOT SINK??? HOW DESPERATE ARE THEY TO TAKE THE SPOTLIGHT AWAY FROM THE GREATEST GAME IN THE WORLD, RUGBY LEAGUE??? I BELIEVE THE WHOLE HUNT KIDNAPPING CAPER IS NOTHING MORE THAN A CON-JOB!!! IT'S A FIT-UP!!! A SLICK MARKETING STUNT!!! IT'S AS FAKE AS THE MOON LANDING IN THE ARIZONA DESERT!!! WAKE UP AND SMELL THE LINAMENT, PEOPLE!!! THESE GUTLESS WONDERS ARE PULLING A WALLABIES JUMPER OVER YOUR EYES!!!

I was interested in Holden McGroyne for a number of reasons. First because he always wrote his columns in capital letters, with three question marks or three exclamation marks after every sentence. And second because his name had turned up in the data I'd copied onto my memory stick from Hunt's laptop. Hunt's daily diary and his itinerary had been on that laptop, as well as his training schedule. By a mysterious coincidence, Holden McGroyne had interviewed Kelvin Hunt on the very same day Hunt's training schedule had been downloaded from his computer. Not only the same day, the same hour. While the interview was taking place, in fact.

I had a third reason to be interested in McGroyne. He used to be on the books at Global Sports Management – Bolivar's company. Back in his playing days with Balmain, McGroyne had employed Bolivar as his marketing agent. McGroyne had retired from the game 15 years ago, but some things – death, taxes, Bolivar – never go away.

So I phoned Holden McGroyne in his

office at the *Daily Herald* in Sydney. He had a reputation for being rude to people who phoned him to waste his time, so I didn't beat around the bush.

'Holden,' I said. 'Fletcher Smith here. Sports detective. I hear you've been selling information on training schedules to the kidnappers of Kelvin Hunt.'

There was a long silence at the other end of the line. A very long silence. Then a choked-up, angry roar. 'What? *What?* Who the hell is this?'

'Fletcher Smith. Sports detective. I'm a big fan of yours.'

'Listen here, you miserable little turd –'

'I'm not the police, Holden. I haven't told anyone what I know. I have certain private interests that I think you can help me with. I believe we may be able to do a deal. Want to talk?'

'I'll talk all right. You just watch me. I'll tell you exactly what I think of your deal, you conniving, blackmailing son of a –'

'Great. Glad to hear that's settled. Nine pm tomorrow at your place, Holden. Don't be late.'

Frank and I drove up from Canberra the following afternoon. Frank was still very worried that no one was paying us to take on the case. I was covering him for petrol on this trip, with money I had left over from the pig's-foot caper, which was my last big job. But there was precious little of that money left. In fact, I was getting so low on cash I had started eating my cereal with a fork to save on milk. I couldn't afford to buy meat, so I'd started going to KFC in the evening to lick other people's fingers.

And the bills for keeping my parents in their private health farm in Switzerland weren't getting any cheaper, either.

'If you want to survive in this trade, you should be doing normal sports P.I. work,' Frank advised me as we hit the outskirts of Sydney. 'You know. Dodgy player transfers.

Drug cheats. Match fixing. Illegal gambling. That was the kind of stuff your father did. All the time. That was the only way he made a living.'

'I know, I know,' I said. 'And I *will* do that stuff. As soon as this Bolivar thing is over.'

Frank shook his head sadly. 'It might never be over, champ. He's a billionaire. No billionaire criminal ever got caught by a 14-year-old kid. You've got your whole life to lead, and you're wasting it on this rubbish. What about school? What about getting an education? Your parents would *kill* me if they knew I was letting you run around like this!'

'I can't go to school with Bolivar still out there,' I said. 'Still living it up. Enjoying the high life, after everything he's done. If you and I don't go after him, who will?'

Just then my mobile rang. It was Inga Brunhoff, my contact inside the Bolivar organisation. Inga was Swiss-German by background. A blackmail scam set up by Bolivar had caused the suicide of Inga's

Australian half-brother, Lawrence Milne, a couple of years ago. Milne was a talented and very handsome basketballer. He had signed with Bolivar, but then realised he was locked into doing beer commercials involving lots of scantily clad girls. Milne was a devout Christian. He refused to do the ads, and insisted on getting out of the contract. In revenge, Bolivar arranged for hundreds of hardcore pornographic images to be 'discovered' on Milne's computer. Maybe Bolivar wanted to use this as leverage to get Milne to sign a new contract, or maybe he simply wanted to ruin Milne's reputation; I don't know. Lawrence killed himself two days before his case went to trial.

Luckily for us, Bolivar had never discovered that Inga and Lawrence were from the same family. They had grown up in different countries. They had different surnames. Different fathers. They had only become close when they'd backpacked around Europe together for a year. That was when Inga had discovered that blood really is thicker than water. Inga had arrived in Australia shortly after Lawrence's death. She was determined to prove it was Bolivar who had planted the porn. But the case never got off the ground. Bolivar was far too clever. The Federal Sports Crime Unit – led by the intrepid Detective Inspector Flintoff – never even got close. So Inga took matters into her own hands, and 'got close' the best way she could.

She became Bolivar's mistress.

She had also been learning English this last year and a half. Unfortunately for the rest of us, she had done all her study at the Ridgy-Didge International School For Dinky-Di Australian English on the Gold Coast. As a result her English was a little . . . *strange*.

'Hoo-roo to my best mate little Aussie battler, Fletcher Smith!' she said when I answered my phone. 'How are you travelling, sport? I am trusting you are bonzer, ya?'

'Very bonzer, thanks, Inga,' I said. 'And you? Keeping well?'

'Ya, I am 'keeping better than Mark Schwarzer! Hahahaha! Zat is zer Aussie football joke! You are getting it, Fletcher, ya?'

'Hilarious, Inga. I'm killing myself.'

'Right now I am relaxing on zer golden sands, soaking up zer rays, watching zer maxed-out surfer-dudes hanging ten in zer gnarly tubes. Blahdy beautiful, mate. Crikey.'

'Any luck with that request I sent you?' I asked.

'Ya, ya. I am checking Samson's Rolodex like you asked. I am looking for zer unusual sings, ya? Sings zat are not zer normal running of zer mule. Plus I am looking for zer names you are giffing me, of zer Willyboys.'

'Wallabies,' I said. 'Yeah, good. And something's come up?'

'Ya, ya. First zer ex-captain, Lachlan Maddox. He was being at a party here six months ago. Just after Hunt got zer coaching job. He and Samson were talking a lot about bikkers.'

'Bikkers?' I leaned into the phone as Frank overtook a truck. 'Was that bikkers, Inga? Are you sure?'

'Ya, ya, bikkers! I am sure as chips! Samson told me himself! Maddox's bruzzer, Cameron, I talk wis Samson about him at zer time, I remember. He is a member of a bikker gang.'

'A bikker gang?' A picture flashed quickly through my mind of a menacing group of hoods, prowling through the city late on a Friday night, squabbling all the time. Then it hit me.

'Oh, a *biker* gang. Like, with motorbikes. OK.'

'Ya, ya, stone zer cobblers, mate! A bikker gang! Also interesting on zis point of view, Samson has been gone to zer bikker racing. A big, big, bikker racing. For zer big bikkers. At Flip Island.'

'Phillip Island,' I repeated. 'That must

have been the Grand Prix back in April. I didn't know Bolivar was into motorsports.'

'I am thinking maybe he goes to talk to some pipple, ya?' Inga said. 'To meet some pipple? Maybe more bikkers?'

'That's terrific, Inga. That gives me plenty to go on. Keep up the good work.'

'Ya. You too, cobbler. Strewth, mate. Maybe soon we put zis blahdy murdering creep behind bars.'

'I hope so. Take care.'

I hung up. Inga had certainly given me lots to think about – in addition to her spectacularly mangled English, that is. Samson Bolivar, one of the richest men in Australia, a globe-trotting sophisticate who surrounded himself with fawning A-list celebrities and dressed in 10,000-dollar suits, hanging out with bikkers – I mean, bikers? Even if Lachlan Maddox's brother Cameron *was* a biker, this didn't make a whole lot of sense.

He could have been arranging a hit on

someone. But normally, Bolivar never met with any of the hit men he employed. It was all done through third parties, out of sight and out of mind. That way, the spotlight never fell back on him.

Could it be that Bolivar had gone to Phillip Island to talk about something more complicated? Something so daring and ambitious that he needed to authorise it personally?

A kidnapping, maybe?

I thought back to when Hunt had been forced into the chopper and abducted. Could Bolivar have enlisted Cameron Maddox and three other bikers to do the dirty deed? It was possible, but somehow it didn't quite ring true. The four men were more like commandos than biker gang members. Their lightning-fast raid had been totally professional. Every movement oozed top-class military training.

And besides, they had all worn exactly the same shoes . . .

'Those bootprints we saw,' I said to Frank. 'They weren't motorcycle boots, were they?'

'No,' Frank said. 'Not a chance.'

'Bolivar's been hanging out with bikers,' I explained. 'Lachlan Maddox's brother is a gang member.'

'Yeah?' Frank said. 'Which gang?'

'Oops,' I grinned sheepishly. 'I forgot to ask her that.'

7. The Badger's Bristle

Holden McGroyne's Sydney residence turned out to be a tiny, single-room bedsit on the second floor of the sleaziest pub in the whole south-west: the Badger's Bristle Hotel. The Badger's Bristle was set two blocks off the main road on a deserted street corner. It was painted the colour of an infected bruise. Inside, at any time of the day or night, you could see a dozen brooding, unshaven men sitting hunched over their tables, staring blankly at the horse races replayed on the mounted TV screens, or licking up spilled beer from the ashtrays.

Upstairs was for sleeping. Downstairs was for drinking. Sometimes the patrons of the Badger's Bristle got the two a little bit confused. Two such confused patrons were outside sleeping soundly on a pile of garbage in the car park as we pulled up. Nice.

McGroyne was a well-paid journo employed by the *Daily Herald*. According to the inside info we'd got from Inga, his wife had divorced him and his kids had grown up and left home. It wasn't just rugby union that he hated, either. He hadn't set foot in his old rugby-league club, Balmain, since it had merged with Wests to become the Wests Tigers a decade earlier. He wasn't poor. Just angry, bitter, and down on his luck. Like a lot of angry, bitter, down-on-their-luck people, he drank.

'It's sad,' Frank said, as we stood at the foot of the outside staircase leading up to the delightful accommodation on the second floor. 'To see a legend of Australian sport living in a place like this. Very sad.'

'Whoa there, Frankie,' I said. 'Don't go all social workery on me again. Please.'

'He used to be a great player,' Frank said.

'I remember watching him in the grand final against the Bulldogs. What a sidestep.'

'Listen,' I said. 'Holden McGroyne is a desperate man. He ran up some gambling debts five years ago and, according to Inga, Bolivar paid them off. I'm guessing Bolivar called in the favour by ordering McGroyne to get an interview with Kelvin Hunt, then copy the training plans for the kidnappers. McGroyne knows he'll go down for this. He could spend the rest of his life in jail. When we go in there, the only reason he's not going to blow my head off is that he'll be too scared *you'll* blow *his* head off *first.*'

We climbed the stairs and found McGroyne's room. There was no answer when Frank knocked on the door. He kept knocking. I was starting to get a bad feeling about this.

'Break it down,' I said.

A well-placed kick from Frank sent the door flying inwards. We stepped into a dank, poorly lit room with a bed along the far wall and a tiny kitchenette with a breakfast bar off to our right. Clothes, magazines, bottles and plates were strewn everywhere. The walls were covered in posters of the Balmain Tigers. A bookshelf was spilling over with books on the club. Other shelves were stuffed full of Tigers memorabilia. Shirts, match balls, trophies, medals, scarves, stuffed toys, photographs – you name it, it was there.

There was a smell in the room that no amount of dirty socks and dinner plates could hide.

Holden McGroyne lay slumped against the base of the breakfast bar. His eyes were wide open. His legs were splayed out in front of him. He had been killed by a single close-range rifle shot to the middle of his chest.

Frank dialled the police on his mobile. After he'd hung up, he took a Turkish army knife (which is just like a Swiss army knife, only bigger and meaner) out of his pocket, and unscrewed the back of Holden

McGroyne's phone. It didn't take him long to find what he was looking for.

'Bugged,' he said, holding up a tiny black bugging device that he had found inside the phone. 'Chances are his work phone was, too.'

'Somebody knew we were coming,' I said. 'And didn't want him to talk.'

'They could still be watching,' Frank said. 'We'd better leave.'

I paused as we headed for the door. I took one last look at the ugly wound in McGroyne's chest. 'What's the rifle?' I asked Frank. 'A .303?'

'No, a .308,' Frank said. 'A biker weapon. The Rebels, the Nomads, the Finks, the Wanderers – they all use it. Looks like our mate Holden was murdered by one of the gang.'

8. John Cougar Melonhead

When we got back to Frank's car, the left rear tyre had been slashed. The passenger door panel had been kicked in. The window above that door had been shattered, and a note had been placed inside on the seat.

'WE KNOW WHO YOU ARE AND WE KNOW WHERE YOU LIVE,' the note said. 'COME NEAR US AGAIN AND YOU ARE A DEAD MAN.'

Frank was not happy. 'Look at this!' he fumed. 'Look at this door panel! And this tyre! I only got new tyres last week!'

'The parking inspectors round here are really aggro,' I said.

'You can joke, little buddy,' Frank

growled. 'They've got my number plate. All they need is contacts in the police, and they can find my name and address easy. *And* nobody is paying us for this job. So who's going to buy me a new tyre, and fix that damage? Huh? Who?'

'I will,' I said.

'Don't be silly. You can't even afford the air that you're breathing.'

Frank didn't have a wife or kids. His car – a Corvette Stingray – was the apple of his eye. He'd earned the money to buy it by taking repeated blows to the head and body from some of the meanest guys ever to step into a boxing ring.

'I'll pay you back for it, I promise,' I said. 'Next time someone gives me a brown paper bag full of money, I'll give you the brown paper bag.'

'Hmph,' Frank scowled. 'If you make any money out of this case, I want half. You and your stupid wild-goose chases. You're turning my hair grey.'

A 50–50 split of the profits was normal between us. That was nothing new. The trouble with this case was that I still had no idea where the money was going to come from. I had been half hoping McGroyne might pay us something to stay quiet about selling Hunt down the river, although given McGroyne's gambling problems and his daily refreshment bill at the Badger's Bristle, I doubted he had anything left in the kitty. And now he was dead. Dead people are notoriously reluctant to part with their cash.

Inga's tip about the bikers was beginning to look like a winner, however. The trail led directly from Hunt to McGroyne to Lachlan Maddox to his brother Cameron, with Samson Bolivar lurking not too far behind.

I had read in the morning paper that Lachlan Maddox was launching a book that same evening, at his luxury penthouse apartment in Woolloomooloo. It was his autobiography, an account of his time as captain of the Wallabies. It was called

Captain Fantastic. It was going to be a big deal, the papers said. Everyone in the A-list sporting party crowd would be there. I felt it would be a terrible waste of a visit to Sydney if we didn't drop by to pay our respects.

Frank was all for heading back to Canberra, so we could lay low for a while. He only had one spare tyre. He couldn't afford to have any more of them slashed.

'You're a private investigator, not a superhero,' Frank lectured me, as we took off the old tyre and put on the new. 'You need to learn the difference. Private investigators don't go around confronting people like Lachlan Maddox for no reason. They stay in the background. They lurk in the shadows. They take photographs. They sift through rubbish bins in the early hours of the morning. They don't walk up to a bloke they think has just murdered someone, introduce themselves, and say "Hello. I think you're the murderer. You or your big bad biker brother better watch out, I'm after you."'

'They do if they need to break the case open,' I said. 'Which we do, Frank. There's no money coming in, and we don't have much time. If we don't get some dirt on somebody soon, we're going to have to walk away.'

'Yeah, and wouldn't *that* be a shame,' Frank sighed.

'Look,' I went on. 'If bikers did kill Holden McGroyne, it's obvious that the Maddoxes were involved. Maybe Lachlan is the link to Bolivar. Maybe he's the one who recommended Cameron for the hit. We're never going to find out if we don't stir things up a little bit. I mean, they're not going to kill us in broad daylight, at their apartment, are they?'

'It's night time,' Frank reminded me.

'OK, but it's a book launch,' I said. 'Think about it. When was the last time anybody got murdered at a book launch?'

'There's a first time for everything,' Frank said.

I'd read a review of Lachlan Maddox's book, *Captain Fantastic*, in the morning paper. Maddox had been a great player in his time – Australia's answer to Jonny Wilkinson. He was a natural fly-half with a great burst of speed and a powerful boot. He could get his team out of trouble with a touch-finding clearance, or win a match in the last minute with a drop-kick from 40 metres. But his personality continually got in the way. After he was made captain, he made the mistake of believing his own publicity. He partied all night, and got into drugs. He married an up-and-coming young starlet, but the marriage hit the rocks even before the good ship *Wedded Bliss* had left harbour. The trouble was, Maddox kept going out to parties and forgetting which up-and-coming young starlet was his new wife.

His on-field performances dropped away badly. When Kelvin Hunt took over the coaching job, the first thing he did was boot Maddox off the team. Privately, Hunt nicknamed Maddox 'John Cougar Melonhead', because of his enormous ego. Somehow this nickname was leaked to the press. Because of this, Maddox not only got sacked, he became a laughing stock. He had more reason than anybody to want Kelvin Hunt dead.

'And the timing couldn't have been worse, with his autobiography coming out,' I said to Frank, as we pulled up in the battered Corvette a block away from Maddox's apartment. 'Poor old Captain Fantastic isn't captain any more. He's not even part of the squad. And John Cougar Melonhead just doesn't quite have the same ring to it.'

'It's still no motive for a kidnapping,' Frank replied. 'Maddox might want Hunt dead, but why would he hold him for ransom? It doesn't make sense.'

'Maybe he's just *helping* the kidnappers,' I said. 'For money. He needs all the money he can get, now that his career is gone.

So he gets his cut, and Hunt disappears, and maybe the new coach will recall Maddox to the captaincy. Maybe all he wants is a new coach, and his spot back on the team.'

We'd got Maddox's address from Inga. I'd also double-checked to make sure Bolivar was not coming to the party. I wanted to shake things up, but not quite *that* much.

Maddox's penthouse apartment was huge, the size of four normal apartments, with a balcony the size of a ballroom overlooking a marina containing a flotilla of million-dollar yachts. A tall, thin bouncer in a white suit and a ponytail was standing guard outside the ground-floor entrance when we arrived.

'And you are . . . ?' he asked us coolly.

'Frank Suleymanoglou,' Frank said. 'The boxer. Lachlan asked me to come.'

Ponytail's eyes widened. 'Frank Suleymanoglou?' he said. 'Really?' Without waiting for an answer he reached out and pumped Frank's hand. 'Hey, sorry, dude.

I knew that. I've seen all your fights, bro. You really rock! Shame about losing to that orangutan, y'know.'

'Panda,' Frank corrected him. 'I lost to the panda. I beat the orangutan. KO'd him in the fifth round.'

'Yeah, right,' Ponytail said. 'I saw that one, too. In that city. With all those canals and gondolas and stuff. Venezuela.'

'Venice,' Frank said. Ponytail didn't ask for invitations. He didn't pay me any attention at all. He stepped to one side, still grinning at Frank, and opened the door to let us in.

A minute later we got out of the lift on the sixth floor, in the lobby leading into the apartment.

It was a touch more upmarket than Holden McGroyne's bedsit at the Badger's Bristle. There was no one lying drunk on piles of garbage or sucking spilled beer from the ashtrays. Sixty or 70 guests were gathered in the living room and out on the balcony. I recognised about half of them. Players, ex-players, coaches, ex-coaches, commentators, sports administrators, TV personalities. There were others who looked familiar, but I couldn't place them until I remembered I'd seen them at a party for business people at Bolivar's house on the Gold Coast, when Bolivar had introduced us to his pet killer jellyfish.

The drinks were flowing freely. Everyone was laughing and talking loudly. Maddox, however, was nowhere to be seen. Frank found himself collared by a young male editor from Maddox's publishing company, who wanted him to write a memoir about his boyhood in Turkey. Frank patiently explained that he had been brought up in the western suburbs of Brisbane, but to no avail.

'C'mon,' the editor said. 'You must have been born in Turkey.'

'Actually, I was born in Ipswich,' Frank said.

'Is that near the Urals?' the editor asked.

I slipped away and went through a door at the end of the living room. It led into a hall. I wasn't looking for anything specific. I was just having a bit of a snoop around. I guess I was secretly hoping that I might find a signed photograph of Bolivar on Maddox's bedside table, with an inscription saying, 'Dear Lachlan. *Thanks for helping me kidnap Kelvin Hunt. Yours, Samson.'* Something helpful like that.

Lachlan's bedroom was at the end of the hallway. At first glance there was no signed photograph inside. The room was disappointingly empty of clues. There was a king-size bed parked against the far wall, a wardrobe off to my right, a small table and chairs, and a home cinema system. That was it. To my left, some vertical blinds had been drawn halfway across an open sliding door, leading out onto another balcony. This was separate from the main balcony, where the party was. The main balcony faced north, out over the harbour, whereas this one faced west, towards another apartment building across the road.

Two men were talking in low voices on the balcony, out past the sliding door. They were standing behind the vertical blinds, so I couldn't see them. But it didn't take me long to figure out who they were. 'Relax, man,' one voice said. 'They can't trace it. There's no way in a million years.'

'They just *did* trace it!' the other voice insisted. 'That's why they phoned McGroyne! They know he's emailed Rory!'

'Nah. They're just guessing.' The first voice remained calm and reassuring. 'They got no proof. They don't know how it was done, Junior. They don't know who McGroyne sent those emails to. I'm telling you, man, there's no way any of it can be traced.'

'That's what you said six weeks ago!' The owner of the anxious voice, Lachlan Maddox, was getting more and more upset. 'And now look! McGroyne's dead! I never signed on for any of this!'

'You're making your cut, so you can just shut your big mouth,' Lachlan's older brother Cameron snapped. 'Leave the clean-up to the experts.'

'Clean-up? Is that what you call it?' Lachlan Maddox scoffed. 'Jeez, Cam. I'd hate to see it when you really make a mess.'

While all this was going on I was standing motionless in the middle of the bedroom, wishing I had a tape recorder. Just as Lachlan finished speaking, the bedroom door opened behind me. The white-suited bouncer from downstairs, Ponytail, stepped in. He stared at me blankly for a few seconds, then closed the door quietly and glanced at the blinds protecting the two Maddox brothers.

'What're you doing here, kid?' he said.

The conversation on the balcony stopped abruptly. Lachlan Maddox swept the blinds aside. He and big brother Cameron walked back through the open sliding door into the room. Lachlan was a big enough bloke, from where I was standing, but Cameron was several sizes bigger. Physique-wise, he was almost a match for Frank. He was dressed in dirty denim jeans, scuffed black biker boots and an armless black leather jerkin, buttoned up at the front, with the word WANDERERS stitched in a circle across the back.

There were only two exits from the room. Both were blocked. I was trapped.

'So what's the story, eh, dude?' Ponytail demanded, fixing his stare on me again. 'What's going on?'

'I was . . . I was just looking for the bathroom –' I backed towards the wardrobe, hoping it might open up and lead me into Narnia. 'But it's not here.'

'Grab him!' Lachlan Maddox ordered.

Ponytail lunged forward. I didn't put up any resistance. There was no point. I let myself be grabbed.

'You know who this kid is?' Lachlan asked.

'He came in with Suleymanoglou,'

Ponytail answered.

'Who?'

'Frank Suleymanoglou. The boxer.'

The look on the two brothers' faces was priceless. I wish I could have bottled it. Their jaws dropped about six floors, right down to ground level and out the front door.

'*Suleymanoglou is here?*' Lachlan Maddox hissed. '*Now?*'

Ponytail blinked. 'Uh, sure, dude. I let him in ten minutes ago. Didn't you invite him?'

'*No I did NOT invite him, you moron!*' Lachlan Maddox clutched at a handful of his golden locks in panic. '*So much for leaving it to the experts!*' he hissed at his brother. '*So much for never being traced! Suleymanoglou's right here in the next room!*'

'Calm down. We'll deal with him.' Cameron Maddox moved behind me to the wardrobe. He slid the door open, reached down, and pulled out an M-16 assault rifle, exactly like the one Hunt's kidnappers had used. 'We deal with him tonight. And the kid, too. I don't know who they're working for, but we have to find out.'

'For God's sake, put that thing away!' Lachlan continued to show his excitable side. I could see why Kelvin Hunt sacked him as captain of the Wallabies. When the heat was on, he melted. His brain turned to mush. *'You can't walk out through my book launch holding an M-16! Are you nuts?'*

'We have to get them out of here,' Cameron shot back. 'Down to the yacht.'

'I can't! I have to give a speech in five minutes! Get him down there yourself!'

With that, Lachlan Maddox stormed out of the room. I was left alone with big brother Cameron and Ponytail. Ponytail had hold of my arm with his left hand, and was digging his fingertips into my bicep. It hurt like hell. I had no idea what was going to happen next, but one thing was for certain. They weren't going to tuck me into bed and sing me nursery rhymes.

9. A Biker's Kiss

Actually, I had a pretty good idea what was going to happen next. Big brother Cameron had pretty much spelled it out for me. He and Ponytail (and maybe Lachlan, if he could get away from the book launch) were going to take Frank and me for a nice little ride on Lachlan's yacht. We would sail out of sight of the coast, at which point the Maddoxes would see what information they could get out of us. Then they would march us up to the bow of the yacht, cut us in half with a burst of sub-machine-gun fire, and feed all four separate halves of us to the sharks.

I had to find Frank. I had to let him know what was happening. He was expecting trouble. He must have noticed me missing by now. Could I risk shouting out to him? Letting him know where I was?

As if reading these thoughts, Cameron Maddox walked right up to me, brandishing the butt of the M-16.

'One peep out of you, punk, and I'll knock your teeth out through your backside. Got it?'

I nodded. Cameron Maddox lowered the rifle again. 'Here's what we do,' he said to me. 'We walk out this door and down the hall. We follow it round *that* way –' He gestured to the left '– till we come to the stairs in the lobby, right next to the lift. We go down those stairs. You, me and my mate Greenie here. Greenie will keep hold of you, nice and tight. And you are not going to make one single sound.'

I nodded a second time. Cameron seemed to relax a little. He opened the wardrobe and put the M-16 back next to Lachlan's dressing gown and slippers.

'Good. Let's go then. And remember. If you even look like making any noise, it'll be lights out. *Kapow!*'

This time he threatened me with a fist. It was a big fist. He had the build of someone who did judo – very muscular around the shoulders and neck. Ponytail (whose real name, it appeared, was Greenie) yanked me towards the door. We walked through and started down the hall.

My mind was racing now. I was computing all the possibilities. What if I didn't yell out? Would Frank figure out what was happening? How long would he wait before he came looking for me? Maybe Cameron *wanted* him to start looking for me, so they could lure him outside onto the yacht and trap both of us.

If I *did* yell, would Frank even hear me? The music at the book launch wasn't as loud as at a nightclub, but it was loud enough. There was a function going on. There were 70 people laughing and talking. I could probably get half a yell in before Cameron Maddox hit me with a biker's kiss and shut me up again. I didn't think half a yell was going to be enough.

I knew one thing for certain. As soon as I stepped out of the apartment and started down the stairs, I was a goner. No one would hear me after that. I *had* to yell. There was nothing else for it. I too a deep breath, and made up my mind to start hollering as soon as we rounded the last corner into the lobby.

We rounded the last corner into the lobby.

I nearly laughed out loud.

There was Frank, directly in front of us. He was standing next to the lift. Right beside the exit to the stairs. Next to him was the editor from the publishing company. The same one who'd wanted a memoir about Frank's childhood in Turkey. Somehow Frank had persuaded the editor to keep him company, as insurance. With the editor in tow there'd be no chance of anything nasty happening.

Cameron swore under his breath. He stopped walking. Greenie and I stopped, too. Cameron glanced back over his shoulder, as if deciding whether or not to return me to the bedroom. He could never get me down to the marina from the sixth floor, however, not unless he tossed me off the balcony. If he did that, I would land face first in the tennis court, for everyone to see.

'Cameron!' Frank exclaimed, grinning as if he'd known Cameron Maddox for years, and had come to the party for a tearful reunion. 'There you are, mate! I got your note. Y'know, the one you left on my car? I've been looking for you all over.'

Frank stepped forward, offering Cameron his hand. Cameron took it. It was a shame I didn't need any diamonds crushed. The force in that handshake would have done it for free.

'Cameron, this is David Middleby from Remainder Publishing,' Frank said. 'I was just telling him about you. There's not a word in your brother's book about you, did you know that? Nothing about how Lachlan Maddox has an older brother who's a member of the Wanderers. David thinks there'd be a huge market for *your* autobiography, too. A book in your own words, telling your own story, about how you turned your back on society, dropped out, and became a biker. Isn't that right, David?'

'Yes!' David said enthusiastically. 'It would be fantastic! Of course, it would need to be ghostwritten, but –'

'You'll get what's coming to you, Suleymanoglou,' Cameron said.

'Me?' Frank replied innocently. 'No, no. I'm not asking for anything. I'm just happy to bring you two together. And I see you've found Fletcher for me, too, eh, Cam? Cheers. We must get together sometime.'

Frank took hold of my right arm. Greenie still had hold of my left. Cameron peered through the archway at the end of the lobby, towards the living room, where Lachlan's book was being launched. Things had suddenly gone quiet in there. The music had been turned down to let Lachlan give his speech. Cameron couldn't do anything to me now without making it very public. His plan to sneak me out down the stairwell to the yacht had just been blown right out of the water.

He nodded tersely to Greenie. Greenie let me go.

10. Sandra At The Four Winds

I guessed we had five minutes. It would take Cameron that long to persuade David Middleby that he had no intention of writing an autobiography, and make his excuses for leaving the book launch. After that, he and Greenie would be all over us like a rash.

We sprinted to the Corvette. And I mean *sprinted*. I've never covered a city block faster in my life. I felt my hamstring twinge alarmingly down the back of my leg as I ran. I'd had three operations on my left knee, after the car accident that nearly killed my parents. I was in the car, too, and got my leg caught in the wreckage. Fortunately, this time nothing tore.

Frank had parked the Corvette down a side road, where it wasn't immediately visible. We got in and took off straight away. As we wound back down the Eastern Distributor towards the airport, I kept an eye out behind us for any approaching Harley Davidsons. My heart skipped a beat when a single powerful headlight pulled out to overtake us, but it wasn't anyone from the Wanderers. It looked like we'd got away.

'That was a close one,' I sighed, turning to face the front again and slumping back in my seat. 'I owe you.'

'Forget it,' Frank said. 'You don't owe me anything. The way you're going, you'll be dead before you're 15.'

'At least we know for sure the Wanderers killed Holden McGroyne,' I said. 'And that Cameron Maddox is pulling the strings. He's doing the dirty work for Bolivar. No doubt about it. He's in on this kidnapping up to his neck.'

'Yeah. But right now it's *our* necks we

need to worry about,' Frank said, glancing for
the hundredth time in the rear-view mirror.
'We need to hole up somewhere in Sydney.
Now. Tonight. We can't risk the open road.'

'Why not?' I said. 'We've got a good head
start. Your Corvette's quick enough.'

'Only if they're chasing us from Sydney,'
Frank said. 'But there are Wanderers in
Canberra, too, you know. There are
Wanderers everywhere. And pretty soon
every single one of them is going to be
gunning for us. We need to lay low.'

I tried to think of somewhere we could
go. I couldn't afford a motel room. Not even
McGroyne's old bedsit at the Badger's Bristle.
I was supposed to be employing Frank, but
I'd already cost him thousands in car repairs,
not to mention hundreds of dollars in hair-
care products, to cover up all those grey hairs
I was giving him. I couldn't ask him to pay.

There weren't many other options. I had
an elderly great-aunt in Sydney who lived
alone and wasn't well. I didn't think she'd

take too kindly to us busting in on her twilight years with a biker gang hot on our tail.

I also had a cousin who lived there, and a few old friends I'd lost touch with since my primary school days, when my parents had lived in Coogee. No one I could trust to let us in and shelter us without asking questions.

Then I remembered someone else. Someone I *could* trust. Someone who *would* shelter us without asking questions.

'What time is it?' I asked Frank.

'8.42,' Frank answered. 'Why?'

'Sandra,' I said. 'She's at Homebush, at a training camp with the AIS squad. It's due to wrap up around about now.'

Sandra Goodnight was a tennis player. She was 15, one of the youngest athletes at the Institute. According to her coaches she had enormous talent, fitness, self-discipline, confidence and personal maturity. She was guaranteed to make squillions of dollars when she turned pro. But I just liked her because of her cute smile.

I hadn't known her that long, but a few months earlier we'd had a romantic near-death experience together involving strapping tape, gym equipment, table-tennis balls, and a hit man named Sparkles McGraw.

Sandra knew my story. She knew why I was obsessed with catching Bolivar. Meanwhile, she was trying to live her own life. In a year or two she would be on the pro circuit, chasing her dream on the big stage, all over the world. We both knew there was no room in her life for a half-baked, under-aged, poverty-stricken sports P.I. with a gammy left leg and a death wish.

But still. You have to have hope.

I called her on my mobile. I heard talking and the clinking of dinner plates in the background when she answered. I figured she must be out somewhere, catching a bite to eat after a hard day double-faulting.

'Sandra, hi,' I said. 'It's Fletcher here.'

'Fletcher, hi!' She sounded pleased to hear from me. 'How're you doing?'

'Not good, Sandra. Not good at all. Tell me. D'you get your own hotel room on this trip?'

There was a pause filled with more clinking of plates. 'I'm sorry? I didn't quite get that.'

'Wherever you're staying for this tennis thing. Do you get your own room?'

'Um, yeah. We always do. I'm at the Four Winds in Parramatta. Why?'

'I need to stay the night,' I said. 'Tonight. It's urgent.'

'Fletcher . . . is this some kind of joke?'

'No. It's no joke. I'm in Sydney and I'm in huge trouble.'

'But I can't let you in! You know that. It's totally forbidden. I'll get kicked off the squad!'

'It's OK, Sandra,' I said reassuringly. 'It's not just me. It's Frank as well. The two of us need to stay. He'll make sure you don't lose your self-control.'

'Yeah, right,' Sandra snorted. 'As if.'

'I'm not kidding, Sandra. None of this is made up. You're our last chance. If you don't help us, right now, we may be dead.'

Now, I ask you: is there any girl who could resist a chat-up line like that? Of course there is, especially if they had half a grain of common sense and a parent listening in on an extension.

'Let me get this straight,' Sandra said. 'If I don't let you into my hotel room, right now, someone's going to kill you?'

'Yes,' I said.

'Who?'

'Some bikers. From a gang called the Wanderers. They just killed a sports journalist named Holden McGroyne. Frank and I found the body, and they're hot on our trail.'

'A sports journalist named *what*?' Sandra said.

'McGroyne,' I repeated. 'Holden McGroyne.'

There was a long pause. 'OK,' Sandra said. 'Now you *have* to be kidding me.'

'No! That's his name! I swear to God!' I should have seen it coming. I should have changed Holden's name to Dick Smith. But now it was too late.

'He's got a column in the *Daily Herald*!' I pleaded. 'He used to play for the Balmain Tigers.'

'You are such a liar, Fletcher Smith. I don't know why I ever listen to you.'

'I'm not lying! Come on, Sandra. Please! You've got to believe me.'

'Why do you have to stay in my room?' Sandra argued. 'Why don't you book your own hotel room somewhere? You've got Frank with you. He can sign in.'

'Because I'm broke,' I said. 'No one's paying me at the moment. The bikers smashed up Frank's car, so I already owe him thousands of dollars. Sandra –'

'All right, all right,' Sandra sighed. 'Honestly, Fletcher. I don't believe I'm doing this. The Four Winds is on Church Street, near the station. I'm in room 501. I'll be back there in about an hour. And be *quiet.*'

11. CHESS TERRORISM

Young aspiring tennis players travel a lot. Not just around Australia, either. If you're at the top, like Sandra, you'll already be playing tournaments in America and Europe when you're 15. If your parents can afford it, you'll be going to private training camps in Florida twice a year. If you're part of the Institute of Sport, you'll be travelling to tournaments constantly. You'll attend six or seven training camps per year. You won't have a weekend to yourself, and neither will your parents, or anyone else who lives with you. Just ask the parents of Roger Federer, Andy Murray or Rafael Nadal. The monster that is the junior tennis circuit takes over your whole life.

At least on this trip Sandra had her own room. It was a nice room, too, with air-conditioning, a TV and a fridge. It was a lot nicer than my room back at the Institute. Because I wasn't a scholarship athlete, I slept on a mattress in my father's office on the third floor of the Sports Commission building. I had no TV or fridge, and showered in a communal shower block with the athletes down at the dorms. I usually ate with Frank or some of the football boys in the Institute canteen. The whole arrangement was only meant to be temporary, until I nailed Samson Bolivar and went back to school, or until my parents recovered enough to come back home from Switzerland. But so far I'd been living in my father's office for more than a year.

We found Sandra's room easily enough. She had showered and changed by the time we arrived. She did not look very pleased to see us.

'Come in. *Quickly*,' she snapped, as she

held open the door. 'I will be in *so* much trouble if anyone sees you here. I must be mad.'

The room had one double bed and one single. I didn't care what the sleeping arrangements were. I'd be happy for Sandra to keep the double, for Frank to take the single and for me to sleep standing up in the shower. At least we had somewhere we could hide safely for the night, and carefully think things through.

Sandra made us a cup of tea while I explained the situation. She'd heard about the kidnapping of Kelvin Hunt, of course. I ran through all the connections from Hunt to Holden McGroyne to the Maddox brothers, and finally to Bolivar.

'If what Inga says is true, and Bolivar met with Cameron Maddox at Phillip Island, then Bolivar is definitely involved,' I said. 'I don't know why he wanted Hunt kidnapped. I don't know who actually kidnapped him. But Bolivar is behind it all.

I'll bet you anything you like.'

'Maybe,' Frank cut in. 'Or maybe not. Bolivar doesn't have to be the mastermind, Fletch. He could just be another link in the chain.'

'What do you mean?' I asked.

'Well, the kidnappers obviously needed guns and a helicopter,' Frank went on. 'Those are not easy things to find. It looks like Cameron Maddox can find them. Bolivar heard about Cameron through Lachlan. He knew Lachlan was weak, and that he hated Hunt for stripping him of the captaincy. So he put the kidnappers in touch with Cameron, knowing Lachlan would never go to the police. The way I see it, maybe the kidnappers offered Cameron a deal. Supply us with weapons. Tidy up for us if things get messy. They paid Lachlan off, just to make sure he stayed quiet. And meanwhile Bolivar fades away into the shadows.'

I thought this over. 'It's possible,' I said. 'Bolivar likes to operate like that, if he can.

Staying in the background, out of harm's way. But what's his motive for getting involved?'

'Who knows?' Frank shrugged. 'Maybe he's got a vendetta against Hunt. Maybe he's betting against Australia in the next World Cup.'

'More importantly,' Sandra said, 'what are the *kidnappers'* motives for being involved? You haven't sorted that out yet.'

'That's a tricky one,' Frank said. 'It's obviously someone who wants Hunt out of the way. Maybe a wealthy diehard rugby fan. Maybe a lone-wolf paramilitary outfit, doing it strictly for the ransom. I don't think it's the Wanderers, though. I agree with Fletcher on that. The Wanderers are strictly low-rent, into drugs and gunrunning.'

'All we have so far is a name,' I said. 'Rory. That's who McGroyne emailed the training sessions to.'

'It's not a lot to go on, is it?' said Sandra.

'No,' I agreed. 'It's not.'

We talked the whole thing around in circles for another hour. Then we turned on the TV to catch the late news. The lead item was about a military coup in the Pacific. Some island called Kiva. A crazy colonel had overthrown the elected government, imposed martial law, and was promising to lead the country to greatness. I didn't catch too much of it, to tell you the truth. International politics has never really been my thing.

The second story was a press conference with Flintoff, about the Hunt kidnapping. Now *that* I understood. I grabbed the remote and turned the volume up a couple of notches. The three of us hung on every word.

Flintoff looked extremely tired. Even the bags under his eyes had bags. He'd lost weight. He no longer looked like he needed towing back out to sea. He looked like he could just about flop back out there by himself.

He was seated at a table somewhere

inside a police station. Lieutenant Calabria was sitting on one side of him. On the other side was an elderly couple I guessed were Hunt's parents.

'We have just received a communication from a group claiming responsibility for the kidnapping of Kelvin Hunt,' Flintoff said. 'Their statement and list of demands is as follows.'

He read from the statement. *'We, the Grand Masters of the Military Wing of the Australian Chess Federation, claim responsibility for the abduction of Kelvin Hunt. The ongoing failure of the Australian government to ratify the International Chess Protocol, officially recognising chess as an Olympic sport, can no longer be tolerated. The failure to fund chess tournaments and youth development programmes is a national disgrace. We will continue to hold Hunt in a safe and secure location until the Australian government ratifies the Chess Protocol and brings funding for chess in line with other major sports. If these demands are not met within a reasonable time, Hunt will be executed.'*

'Wow,' I said to Frank and Sandra, when Flintoff had finished reading. 'Chess terrorism. That's a first.'

'Chess players can get pretty intense,' Sandra said.

'The Grand Masters of the Military Wing,' I repeated. 'Sounds like a secret order. I wonder how they'll execute him. Pawn to queen four?'

'It wouldn't be so funny if they *did* execute him,' Sandra said.

'They won't,' I said. 'It's a bluff. It's got to be. I mean, what have chess players got to be murderous about? So they don't go to the Olympics! Neither do boogie-board riders! Big deal!'

'The way chess is treated in this country is terrible,' Frank said. 'It's the prince of sports. It's the most difficult game there is.'

'But that's exactly my point,' I said. 'It's a *game*, not a sport. It's like cards, for example.

Bridge is not a sport. Poker is not a sport. Sport means people are hitting each other. They're throwing things. Or kicking things. Or running somewhere. You know. *Moving.'*

'You don't think poker's a sport?' Sandra said.

'Are poker players athletes?' I retorted.

Sandra cleared her throat. 'The ones on TV certainly aren't,' she said.

'And they're the good-looking ones,' I said. 'Of course poker players aren't athletes. They're slobs. They're late-night, knuckle-dragging tryhards. If they were still living at home, their parents would lock them in the laundry with some washing powder and some dental floss. Most of them are so unfit they can't even lift their own money.'

'Chess players are different from poker players, Fletcher,' Frank pointed out.

'You're right,' I agreed. 'They certainly are. Chess players don't *make* any money.'

Frank sighed. 'It's Neanderthals like you

who have forced these poor people from the military wing of the Chess Federation to take radical action,' he said. 'If they kill Kelvin Hunt, it'll be all your fault.'

12. Stirring Things Up

Frank and I ended up sharing the double bed. Sandra took the single. As I drifted off to sleep, my mind grappled with another problem we hadn't solved. Where exactly *was* Hunt? Was he really in the hills west of Coffs Harbour, as Flintoff and the Sports Crime Unit supposed? If so, how had the kidnappers escaped with him in their helicopter so easily? Frank and I had clearly seen them leaving Coffs Harbour heading west. Other witnesses in town had heard them go that way, too. They'd made such a lot of noise, you'd think Flintoff could easily have tracked their movements and discovered their hide-out. Unless . . . Unless they'd gone west to throw everyone off the scent.

What if they'd headed that way, with chopper blades chopping and red lights flashing, then found a way to take Hunt somewhere else entirely?

I had other problems to worry about next morning. I could *not* decide whether to have the cooked breakfast or the continental. In the end I had both. One of each. It felt great to eat my cereal with a spoon for a change, instead of a fork.

We sat in the hotel lobby with Sandra while she waited for the team bus to take her to her last day of training. Most of her squad were still eating breakfast together, at a table in the far corner of the room. A few girls, like Sandra, were sitting with relatives or friends, so we didn't look conspicuous. Or at least I didn't. Frank always looked conspicuous. He drew a few curious glances from passers-by. Fortunately none of these glances belonged to anyone who wanted to gun us down.

'So what's on the agenda for today?' I asked Sandra, as I sipped on a coffee so strong it kept jumping out of the cup to do push-ups. 'Volleying into the net? Backhand errors? Or more double-faulting?'

'We've got the guys from the Davis Cup team coming in to give us a few pointers.'

'Right,' I nodded. 'Like how to hit the ball inside the court.'

'You're just jealous, Fletcher. Admit it.'

'Of course I'm jealous,' I said. 'Look at this place. Cooked breakfast. All the coffee you can drink. Air-conditioning. TV in your room. Mini bar stocked with chocolate. Do you think Tennis Australia would mind if Frank and I stayed another couple of weeks?'

'Why don't you ask them?' Sandra said.

'We can't go back to Canberra, can we?' I said to Frank. 'We can't go anywhere. Except maybe to Flintoff, and he won't believe a word we say.'

'We're going to have to catch them, Fletcher,' Frank said gloomily. 'Just the two of us. All by ourselves.'

I was shocked. Frank was normally

the one urging caution. Holding me back. Cramping my style. Hearing him say we should go after the bad guys by ourselves was like hearing a pig telling a butcher how to make bacon.

'Steady on there, Frank,' I said. 'What happened to staying in the background? Lurking in the shadows? Sifting through garbage bins, that kind of thing?'

'You've got Bolivar's mobile number, haven't you?' Frank said. 'Call him.'

'What, you mean now?'

'I mean right now.'

I was shocked again. I'd heard of putting your head in the lion's mouth, but this was ridiculous. Ring Bolivar? When we had no proof he was involved? What good would that do?

I did have Bolivar's private number, though. Inga had given it to me. I was very reluctant to use it, for two reasons. First because Bolivar would change it immediately if I did. Second, he might start to wonder how such an important item of personal information came to be in my possession, which could put Inga straight into the firing line.

'We have to stir things up,' Frank said. 'If we don't, we're dead men. We don't have much time.'

A little reluctantly, I fished out my mobile phone and found Bolivar's number. I called it. Bolivar answered after three rings.

I took a deep breath. 'Samson,' I said. 'Fletcher Smith here. Can you talk?'

He could have hung up. I was half-expecting him to. But his curiosity got the better of him, and he didn't.

'Young Fletcher,' he said, in his smooth, deep baritone. 'How nice to hear from you. I'm about to go in to a meeting, my friend. I hope this isn't one of your aimless rants.'

You had to give it to him. The man could handle himself superbly well. If the Bolivars had a family motto, it would be 'Charming Unto Death'. Making him sweat was harder than teaching a cockatoo to speak Swahili.

'I understand you were at Phillip Island last year,' I said. 'I didn't know you were into motorsports. Are you still following the bikes?'

'No, sadly,' Bolivar replied. 'My interest in motorsports has come to an end.'

'Sure,' I said. 'What with the failure of the Wallabies in the World Cup, and the value of all your players decreasing, I suppose a lot of your time is devoted to that.'

There was a split-second pause. Not long enough for anyone else to notice, which was a shame. I'd activated the record function on my mobile phone. The conversation was being recorded. But of course Bolivar would know that.

'I did have players involved, yes,' he said. 'And I love the game dearly, so naturally I was concerned. Fletcher, why have you called? I really don't have time for this.'

'Neither do I,' I replied. 'I've got Cameron Maddox and the Wanderers after me. They tried to kill me last night, Samson. Me and Frank. After we found Holden McGroyne's body. They're desperate to bump me off before I can get to Rory.'

Another split-second pause. Again, not long enough to mean anything. Not to anyone but us.

'I have no idea what you're talking about,' Bolivar said calmly.

'Oh, yes, you do.' I soldiered on. 'You met Cameron Maddox at Phillip Island. Not long before Kelvin Hunt was kidnapped. I think that's how Cameron got to know Rory. I think Cameron and Rory cut a deal to supply the hardware for the kidnapping. I think Cameron also signed on at that meeting to be the security. He murdered McGroyne because he was threatening to spill the beans to the papers. I also think you're in this one up to your neck, Samson, which means you must be planning to make money out of it somehow. I just wish I could figure out how.'

'I think you've been playing too much PlayStation,' Bolivar said. 'Goodbye.'

The line went dead. I flipped my phone shut, and returned it to my pocket. I had no idea whether the conversation had achieved anything, apart from letting Bolivar know we were hot on his trail. No doubt he would contact Cameron Maddox, and suggest very strongly that Maddox hurry up and finish us off.

Just stirring things up, like Frank asked me to.

Just following orders.

13. Can i Fax You A Footprint?

Frank's plan was to return to Woolloomooloo, to shadow Cameron Maddox. We would be following him while he was looking for us. That sounded like a recipe for something to happen *very* quickly. Hopefully something that would lead us to the kidnappers, and to Bolivar. Or else to an early grave.

Frank couldn't be seen driving the Corvette. We needed to hire a different car for a few days. Expense was piling on expense, and money was draining out of my account faster than rats leaving a sinking ship.

Frank ended up paying for the car. It was a V8 Commodore. Common enough to blend in, yet powerful enough to match it with the Wanderers' Harleys. Not bulletproof, though. Unfortunately, the car hire companies were fresh out of bulletproof V8 sedans.

'If we need to stay any more nights, I'll pay,' Frank said, as we drove through the Cross City Tunnel under William Street on our way east. 'Unless you've got more girlfriends in fancy hotels.'

We found a park near a children's playground set back from the marina. Instead of watching Maddox's apartment, we watched the yachts. If Cameron was involved in gunrunning – particularly M-16s, which are not standard issue in the Australian Army – then Lachlan's yacht was probably the transport. Using that, he could meet with boats off the coast, under cover of darkness, and bring the weapons secretly back to shore.

'And meanwhile Lachlan turns a blind eye for a cut of the profits,' I said, shaking my head. 'To think he was captain of the Wallabies. I used to idolise him. It's enough to make me a cynic. If I wasn't so cynical already.'

'Kelvin Hunt saw right through him, though,' Frank said. 'He sacked him after one week. I think I'm starting to respect Kelvin Hunt.'

'Yeah, he's no mug,' I said. 'Under all that bluff and bluster I think he might be a pretty fair judge of character. Except for the fact that he hired you.'

We watched the marina all morning. There was no sign of movement in or out. At midday, a news bulletin on the car radio told us that former Wallabies' coach Tim Jamieson had been reappointed until Hunt's return. Lachlan Maddox had been recalled and reinstated as captain.

Five minutes later, I got a call from Lieutenant Calabria. She was back in Canberra with Flintoff, trying desperately to put all the pieces of the puzzle together.

So far, she was failing miserably.

'What do you know about Lachlan Maddox?' she asked me. 'Did you hear he's just been reinstated as Wallabies' captain?'

'I heard it on the news just then,' I said. 'I know he's involved in gunrunning and murder, but only as an accomplice. His older brother Cameron is the big cheese. Cameron killed Holden McGroyne yesterday with a .308. He either did it himself, or ordered it done. You're probably on the McGroyne case by now, aren't you? Has that one been referred to you?'

'Yes,' Lieutenant Calabria replied. 'Yes, it has. But how did you –?'

'McGroyne had passed on the Wallabies' training schedules at Coffs Harbour to the kidnappers. He was going to spill the beans. That's why he got killed. Cameron's running M-16s as well as rifles, and an M-16 was used by the kidnappers when they snatched Hunt. Lachlan's in on it all, but Cameron pays him off to keep him quiet.

Now that McGroyne is dead, Lachlan's getting pretty jumpy. Actually, Cameron's getting jumpy, too, judging by last night. He tried to bump Frank and me off in the middle of a book launch.'

'You were at Lachlan's book launch?' Without waiting for an answer, Lieutenant Calabria continued. 'Where are you now?'

'In a rented Commodore, watching his yacht.'

'Do we know who the contact is for the kidnappers? The one McGroyne was in touch with?' the lieutenant asked.

'No, it was some bloke named Rory,' I said. 'That's all I know at the moment. I'm working on it.'

'Rory?' Lieutenant Calabria repeated.

'Yes. Rory. No surname. Just Rory. Maybe he's the head honcho, I'm not sure. I think he was introduced to Cameron Maddox by Bolivar.'

I went over the details a few more times until I was sure Lieutenant Calabria had them. It wouldn't hurt to have someone at the Canberra end, turning some screws. What I wanted most of all was for Flintoff to get serious and start mounting a proper surveillance operation on Bolivar. They needed to bug his phones. Bug every room in his house. Follow him wherever he went. That would relieve the pressure on Inga, and make sure her cover stayed safe. It would also be the quickest way to find out Rory's identity, and find out who was behind this whole sorry mess.

But Flintoff wouldn't move on him until it was too late.

'Tomorrow we're going to come after Lachlan,' Lieutenant Calabria told me. 'He's our main suspect, now that he's got the captaincy back. That gives him a clear motive. Of course, he'll *know* he's a suspect, so he'll be playing it very cool. I'll tell Flintoff about Cameron, and about McGroyne. That should help.'

'Don't mention me as a source,' I said.

'Please. If you do, Flintoff will laugh in your face.'

I was about to hang up when I remembered something. 'Listen,' I said. 'This may not be important. But can I fax you a footprint?'

'A footprint?' the lieutenant said. 'What sort of footprint?'

'I took a footprint off the training ground at Coffs Harbour. It's just a drawing, not a proper imprint. But it's a pretty good likeness. I've got it with me here. I can't figure out what sort of boot it is, and neither can Frank. Maybe you'll have better luck.'

There was a print shop in the next suburb. I photocopied the footprint and faxed it to Lieutenant Calabria in Canberra. Then, for the rest of the afternoon, Frank and I watched the entrance to the marina. We were staking everything on Cameron turning up eventually. As soon as we knew which yacht was Lachlan's, we could turn it over to the Sports Crime Unit, or maybe search it ourselves. I had a hunch there would be money stashed on board that yacht. Guns. Maps. Supplies for long trips out to sea. It was Cameron's HQ for his gunrunning operation. It probably had been for years.

'He'll try and get his stuff off it before the police arrive,' I said to Frank, just after nine o'clock that evening, when we were both thinking of quitting. 'He'll know they're closing in.'

'Maybe he's got his stuff already,' Frank said. 'He could have done that when he heard the news.'

'Yeah, but that was midday,' I replied. 'We were already here by then. And we haven't seen a thing.'

'That was when the news broke on *radio*,' Frank corrected me. 'Cameron could have been told much earlier. Maybe last night, when we were holed up at the Four Winds. That would have given them all night to load up and drive away.'

This prospect didn't make me feel any

better. If Cameron had already cleaned out the yacht, the SCU would find nothing. No M-16s. No stashes of money. No supplies. No maps. No rifle that could have been used to kill Holden McGroyne.

'We have to find that yacht. Now,' I said finally. 'If it's empty, we're sitting in the wrong place.'

'Agreed.' Frank nodded and opened the car door. 'Let's go.'

14. Fish Food

The marina had lots of yachts in it. At first glance, there was no way of telling which one belonged to Lachlan Maddox. It was like looking for a needle in a needlestack. They all seemed pretty much the same. Fortunately, Lachlan's enormous ego had made it easy for us. After searching for five minutes, we found a yacht named *Captain Fantastic*. Oh yes, I thought. That just *had* to be his.

The *Captain Fantastic* was a luxury two-masted ketch, 25 metres long. She was the same size as the maxi yachts in the Sydney to Hobart, although she was built for comfort, not for speed. Nevertheless, with a decent breeze filling her two big sails,

I guessed she would clip along at a fair old pace. You could sail around the world in a yacht like that. Easy. Smuggling loads of semi-automatic weapons from cargo ships or other yachts out beyond Australia's territorial waters would be child's play.

She was moored right at the end of the marina. We were well away from the lights at the marina entrance and the glow of the apartment buildings and streetlamps beyond. There were no lights on in the cabins of any of the other yachts, either, which was good news for us. If we wanted to break into the *Captain Fantastic* to have a bit of a look, we could do so in private, away from prying eyes.

Frank had brought a spanner with him from the boot of the Commodore. He had wrapped the head of it in a towel, so he could break one of the yacht's windows. He was eyeing up which window would be best to smash when I spotted something. A shadowy figure crouched down in the stern of a trailer-sailer, 20 metres back along the jetty.

'Hold it, hold it,' I said, as quietly as I could. 'We've got company.'

The man slowly stood up. Another man stood up beside him. Two more men started climbing down from the top deck of a game-fishing boat opposite.

One, two, three more men appeared. I was amazed. We hadn't spotted anybody when we were looking for Lachlan Maddox's yacht. But then, we hadn't been looking for people. We hadn't paid any attention to shapes lurking in dark corners.

'You know, it's a funny thing,' I said to Frank, as the men stepped off the yachts and onto the jetty. 'The boats in this marina are all owned by big ugly fat blokes in biker boots. And they all have beards.'

They were all dressed the same, too – in denim and dark leather. Some were carrying baseball bats. One was holding a long piece of metal pipe. We had obviously stumbled on a late-night meeting of the Royal Bearded Plumbers and Fat Ugly Baseballers Yachting Association. And they didn't want us to join.

The cabin door of the *Captain Fantastic* opened behind us. I turned to see Cameron Maddox smiling at me. It wasn't a friendly smile. In fact, I'd seen warmer smiles on a ghost train. Somehow, Maddox had set a trap for us. He and his biker mates had been waiting all day for us to come snooping. The Woolloomooloo chapter of the Royal Bearded Plumbers and Fat Ugly Baseballers Yachting Association was about to call its meeting to order.

They kept advancing on us. Slowly. Biding their time. We backed away to the very end of the jetty, at the furthest point from the shore. Then we stopped. We had nowhere left to run.

'End of the line, boys,' Cameron Maddox said to us. 'Your tour of the bottom of Sydney Harbour is just leaving. Looks like you've already met your crew.'

'The tinnie!' Frank hissed, nodding to my right. 'There! To your right! Go!'

A small, lightweight aluminium dinghy had been stowed in the stern of a luxury cruiser beside me. I could just see a set of oars poking up dimly from the bow. Frank and I leapt on board the cruiser and began wrestling with the ropes that were tying the dinghy down.

'Get it in the water!' Frank yelled. 'Quick!'

He dodged a whistling baseball bat and kicked out at one of the bikers as I fumbled with the wet rope. A second man attacked him from the side, but was met with a spanner to the head and went flying. I hauled the dinghy into the water and sprang down into it, as suddenly there were Bearded Plumbers and Fat Ugly Baseballers swarming all around the cabin. Frank was looking like he could use a bit of a hand.

'Frank! Jump!'

'It's all right, mate. There're only ten of them. Row!'

He decked a couple more while he was talking. I fitted the rowlocks into their holes on the sides of the dinghy, and pulled with the oars as hard as I could. With a grunt, Frank laid a perfect shoulder charge on one last pipe-wielding biker, then dived off the edge of the stern. He hit the water with an almighty splash, came up spluttering beside me, and nearly capsized us by hauling himself aboard.

I handed him the oars, then shuffled to the stern. Frank rowed hard towards the open harbour. None of the Wanderers had jumped in the water after us. They seemed to have disappeared. Our best hope was to lose them in the darkness, then find somewhere safe to land in an adjacent bay.

Frank kept rowing. I took in some deep breaths to calm down. Things were looking a lot better than they had done a minute earlier. Back then we were odds-on to end up as sharkbait. Maybe we'd done enough to escape.

The high-pitched roar of a motorbike engine broke into my thoughts.

Another roar followed it. Then another. And another.

But I was wrong. They weren't motorbike engines. Moments later, only just visible in the milky haze along the foreshore, four sleek black metal tubes came sweeping out from behind the marina, leaving long luminescent trails on the water.

'Jet skis!' I howled. '*Harley Davidson* jet skis! Row, Frank! Row like the wind!'

'Row yourself,' Frank groaned. 'I'm done in.'

'Hurry, Frank! They're gaining!'

'Of course they're gaining, you halfwit!' Frank hissed. 'They're 800 ccs!'

He was right. Not even Frank the Turk could out-row a jet ski. It was like a slug trying to out-wriggle a Ferrari. It just couldn't be done.

Cameron Maddox was driving the lead jet ski. As he got closer I saw a rifle nestled snugly across his lap. It was possibly the same rifle that had killed Holden McGroyne. If not, it was a close living relative. I had no doubt it could make the same big, messy hole in my chest.

Frank stopped rowing as the jet skis drew alongside. There was no point in going any further. The game was over and we had lost.

Fish food, here we come.

'I'm disappointed in you, Suley-manoglou!' Cameron said. 'You quit!'

'We're in a dinghy,' I said crossly. 'You didn't give us a chance!'

'Sure I did,' Cameron said. 'I could've blown your head off back at the marina.'

'You could have chased us in a surf ski,' I retorted. 'Or a kayak. You could have dived in and swum after us. But no. You had to cheat. You had to use *engines*.'

'Kid,' Maddox leaned forward towards me. 'This isn't Little Athletics. I'm playing to win.'

'Here's the pick-up now, Cam,' one of

the jet-ski riders interrupted.

'Great.' Maddox glanced out towards the open harbour. 'Right on time.'

I followed his gaze, squinting into the half-darkness ahead of us. Amidst the confusion of shadows and green-and-red twinkling sea lights I could just make out the shape of an enormous luxury cruiser nosing past the headland into the bay. It was one of those oversized floating fibreglass wedding cakes that are called yachts, even though they've never run up a sail.

'What's that, the *Queen Mary*?' I said.

'Yeah, kid.' Cameron Maddox picked up his rifle. 'And I'm the King of France. Now start rowing.'

15. A Marriage Made in Heaven

It took us a further 20 minutes to reach the wedding cake. It was a lot further away than it looked. With each metre we receded from shore, I figured our chances of survival grew slimmer.

Eventually, we pulled up alongside the cruiser. Two floppy plastic ladders led up the side of the hull from the water's edge to the deck. Frank shelved the oars, while Cameron Maddox watched us like a hawk.

'Guns,' Maddox said. 'Hand them over. Now.'

Frank took his black .38 Beretta out of his holster and gave it to Maddox. I didn't carry a pistol. I didn't know how to shoot straight for a start and, worse than that, I didn't trust myself to make the right decisions. If I'd carried a gun, I probably would've started shooting back at the marina, which would've been a big mistake. Frank knew that. That's why we were still alive.

Maddox let out a piercing whistle. A figure appeared at the top of the ladders, holding what looked like a pump-action shotgun. Another figure holding another shotgun appeared beside him. These boys certainly did like their guns. Their comrades-in-arms down at sea level stayed perched on their jet skis, bobbing up and down next to the hull. It was quite a welcoming party. The only thing missing was a regiment of Royal Scots Guards to pipe us aboard.

We climbed the ladder. The crew at the top opened a door in the side of the cabin and ushered us through. Frank went first, ducking his head to avoid the doorframe. I followed. I had just stepped onto some carpet when someone standing just inside the door brought down something hard and heavy onto the back of my head, and I knew no more.

I woke with a dry taste in my mouth and a very sore head. The dry taste in my mouth was due to the air-conditioning. The sore head was due to being welcomed aboard with a crack to the back of the skull.

I was lying in my clothes on a bunk bed in a small cabin. Frank was sitting on a chair nearby. His expression suggested that our situation had not improved. The cabin was OK, however. It looked like staff quarters. It contained a small TV, a DVD player, a mini bar, a two-seater lounge and a bathroom. All in all, not much worse than Sandra Goodnight's room at the Four Winds.

I sat up. My head felt like a vase that had just been smashed. It was good to see Frank, but right then I needed to be fussed over. I needed to be tended. I needed to be comforted and told everything would be all right. In other words, I needed my mother.

For a split second – or maybe two split seconds, or even three – I felt extremely sorry for myself. No parents. No money. No breaks in the case. Even worse, it looked like we'd fallen into the evil clutches of the Grand Masters of the Military Wing of the Chess Federation.

The endgame was about to begin.

'Hey, Sport,' Frank said – which was about as close as he ever came to fussing over me. 'How you feeling?'

'Great,' I said. 'My head just *loves* having my skull split open. Are we locked in?'

'Yep.'

'So . . . we're prisoners?'

'Correct again.'

'How long have I been knocked out? Is it morning yet?'

'Uh huh. It's just past eight o'clock.'

As I talked, I checked in my pockets for my mobile. It was gone. So was my wallet. In my back pocket I found something completely unexpected: a tiny, flat, circular metal object about the size of a five-cent coin. As I held it in my hand, it gave off a series of dull red flashes.

'A tracking device,' I said. 'How long has *that* been there?'

Frank took it from me and studied it. 'I'd say two nights. Since the book launch.'

'Right,' I nodded. 'Cameron Maddox dropped it in my pocket when he dragged me down the hall. That's how he knew we were at the marina.'

'All the time we were watching them, they were watching us,' Frank said. 'Watching them watching us. Watching –'

I shut my eyes. Sometimes you just get the feeling that the whole world is working against you. When were we going to stop going around in circles, chasing our tails? Probably not till these fiendish chess terrorists set our feet in concrete and dropped us to the bottom of the ocean.

At least then we'd be going in a straight line.

'I'd give anything to know who's behind all of this,' I sighed. 'Is it really the Chess Federation? Or whatever they call themselves – the Military Wing? Did they organise the kidnapping and order McGroyne to be killed? If I knew that, I reckon I could die happy.'

'It's not the Chess Federation,' Frank said casually, as if this was the most obvious thing in the world. 'That was just a smokescreen.'

'Sorry?' I said. 'What was that again?'

'It's the Kivanese. The new government. The one that staged a coup last week.'

I stared at him. 'You mean that mad Pacific island colonel we saw on TV?' I said. 'What was his name again?'

'Sisimarama,' Frank said. 'Colonel *Rory* Sisimarama. Supreme Leader of the Kivanese Armed Forces. Prime Minister of Kiva – as of last Wednesday. *And* diehard rugby fan.'

'Holy cow,' I said. 'So . . . hang on . . . *he's* the one who kidnapped Hunt? So Hunt could coach the Kivanese national team?'

'That's right.'

'No.' I shook my head. 'It can't be right. It's nuts.'

'Not if you think about it,' Frank continued. 'If you think about it, it all makes perfect sense. The Kivanese love their rugby. It's their national sport. They're a fast-running attacking team, with a terrible defence. Their line-outs are a shambles. Their scrums are a joke. And Hunt's great strengths are –'

'Defence, line-outs and scrums,' I said. 'It's a marriage made in heaven.'

'The Kivanese always do brilliantly at rugby sevens,' Frank went on. 'They even won a World Cup, about 15 years ago. They're consistently ranked in the world top five. But in proper rugby, 15 a side, they never get anywhere. They didn't get past the first round in the World Cup earlier this year. I think, for the colonel, that was the last straw.'

'He cares about rugby that much?' I said.

Frank smiled. 'When Kiva won the sevens World Cup,' he said, 'Guess who was captain of the team?'

I took a long shot. 'Colonel Rory Sisimarama?'

'You got it in one.'

I rubbed my eyes again. Things were slowly beginning to fall into place. The Grand Masters of the Military Wing of the Australian Chess Federation were fakes. The whole thing was nothing but a ruse, designed to throw Flintoff and the Sports Crime Unit off the scent. The paramilitaries who'd kidnapped Hunt weren't Australians at all. They were Kivanese commandos. And they weren't holed up in the bush out the back of Coffs Harbour. Somehow, they'd managed to whisk Hunt out of the country. They'd probably taken him all the way back to Kiva.

So all this time Flintoff had been searching for Hunt on the Dorrigo Plateau,

Hunt had been imprisoned on a tropical island. Living on dates and coconut milk. Coaching the Kivanese national team.

'But . . . Hunt *can't* coach the Kivanese national team,' I said. 'If he ever turns up at a game, everyone will know what happened. The Kivanese can never take him anywhere.'

'Sure,' Frank said. 'Hunt can't physically leave the country. But he can coach the team right up till they leave. And after that, he can stay in touch. He can watch the games on video. He can talk to the team at half-time. It's crazy, it's all totally crazy, but it could work.'

'Hunt's a great motivator,' I said. 'They could start causing a few upsets. Beat Australia maybe. Wow. Wouldn't *that* put a few noses out of joint! It could be the upset of the century.'

'And that's exactly what Sisimarama's counting on,' Frank said. 'He wants glory for his country. Nothing else will do. Right now, his military government is in big trouble.

There are protests. People marching in the streets. Everyone's demanding the return of democracy. But how much opposition do you think there'll be if the country's heroes start doing well?'

'None.' I laughed. 'Sisimarama will be a hero, too.'

'And the only thing stopping him,' Frank said, 'is us. Because now we know everything. We're the only ones standing in his way.'

I nodded. Something occurred to me that probably should have occurred to me earlier, but my head was busy screwing itself back on.

'So . . . Frank . . . why aren't we dead?' I said. 'And how come we know all this stuff? How'd you find it out? Who told you?'

'Bolivar,' Frank shrugged. 'Who else?'

16. BOLIVAR

Bolivar. Naturally. It was his yacht that we were being held prisoner on. Bolivar was on the yacht, too, enjoying a little break from running his evil empire while we steamed, full speed ahead, towards Kiva. Frank had already met with Bolivar while I'd been sleeping. According to Frank, we were being kept alive for one reason, and one reason only: Colonel Sisimarama wanted Frank to work with the team.

I had to laugh when I heard that. I laughed so hard my head started to hurt again. 'So the colonel is a big fan of yours?' I said. 'You sure pick 'em.'

'He's not a *fan*,' Frank said uncomfortably. 'This is strictly business. The colonel asked

Hunt who was the best sports conditioner in Australia. And Hunt recommended me. So here I am.'

'But what about me?' I said. 'I'm no sports conditioner. I'm not even a sports shampoo. How do I fit into all of this?'

'You're the insurance,' Frank said. 'If I don't work with the team, they kill you. They shoot you in the back of the head. And I get to watch.'

I took a shower to try to freshen up. The hot water felt great, but then I had to put back on my wonderfully fragrant three-day-old clothes. Mmmm. Those clothes smelled good. They fitted me like used clingfilm. Another couple of days without a wash, and they would start to dissolve my skin.

I looked at myself in the mirror, mustering as much courage as I could. Bolivar was waiting on the top deck. I couldn't let the good captain down. If I was lucky, he might tell me a jolly seafaring yarn and let me steer the boat towards Kiva for a while.

After I'd got dressed, I walked with Frank up some stairs and along a corridor to the main lounge. Bolivar was sitting at a polished dark-wood table, alone in the enormous room. There was lots of dark wood, and lots of leather. A bar laden with bottles of wine and spirits gleamed in the corner to my left. A huge LCD TV screen was mounted on the wall to my right, but nothing was on.

Bolivar looked impeccable in an open-necked white shirt and white trousers. A hint of gold flickered on his wrists, around his neck, and on several fingers. He was relaxing on a plush leather sofa, sipping on a whisky, enjoying each small taste to the full.

'Fletcher,' he said. 'Come and join us.'

Frank and I made our way to the table and sat down. I was just beginning to wonder who the 'us' was when a door behind Bolivar opened. Inga Brunhoff walked in.

It took all my self-control not to react.

The rush of adrenalin through my veins was so strong it nearly floored me. They say there is a moment just before an earthquake when you *know* the ground is going to open up and swallow you. That was what I felt like right then.

'Inga, this is Fletcher Smith,' Bolivar said. 'Fletcher, Inga Brunhoff. I believe you two know each other.'

The ground started to open up. I stared into Inga's eyes. She stared back into mine, showing no expression. For a second my heart seemed to stop beating.

'I don't tink so,' Inga said, with perfect contempt. 'I don't hang out wis kids.'

'Didn't you meet at my place last year?' Bolivar said. 'When Fletcher gatecrashed my party?' He suddenly burst out laughing. 'Oh no. So sorry. That was my wife.'

The crack in the earth closed again. My heart jump-started. I stared at Bolivar's whisky. At the blank TV screen. Out the windows. Anywhere but at Inga.

'You should not be bringing babies on zis trip, Samson,' Inga said, in that same haughtily dismissive tone.

'I didn't invite him,' Bolivar replied. 'I never invite him. He just has a habit of turning up.'

'Well, throw him overboard zen,' Inga shrugged. 'Leave him on an island. Get rid of him. He cramps our style.'

'Pour me another whisky, will you, my dear?' Bolivar said, handing her his glass. 'Thanks.'

'A large one,' I added. 'A triple.'

'No, no,' Bolivar laughed. 'A small one please. Just a finger.'

Inga poured the drink, then announced she was going up to the top deck, 'to soak up zer rays.' There was silence for a while once she had gone. Outwardly I was calm, but inside I was boiling. Bolivar always had that effect on me. Every day of my life I thought about putting him behind bars for what he had done to my parents. For what he had done to Inga's half-brother, as well as countless other victims. Bolivar sailed through life like he sailed to Kiva – in grand style, without a care in the world. Meanwhile, everyone else paid.

'You must learn to control your tongue, Fletcher,' Bolivar said. 'I could make life very unpleasant for you, if I wished.'

'So what?' I said. 'You're going to kill us anyway.'

'Perhaps. But here you are, on a ten-million-dollar yacht, sailing to a tropical island paradise. You are part of a most unusual enterprise. I'm sure your friend Frank has explained some of what is happening. We are writing a new chapter in the history of the great Pacific island nation of Kiva. You should have a sense of occasion, at least.'

'Sorry,' I said. 'Next time you kidnap me I'll be more grateful.'

'I'm afraid there won't be a next time,' Bolivar said firmly.

So he *was* going to kill us. Well, let's face it, it was the sane and sensible thing to do. He could hardly let us go, considering everything that we knew. I doubted we had anything to fear from him personally, or any of the crew working on his yacht. He was simply handing us over to the colonel. It would be the Kivanese military who would finish the job.

As soon as Frank's gig with the national team was over, we were history. I doubted we would even get to see them play their first game.

17. Rendezvous

Kiva is made up of more than 200 islands. The two largest, Kiva Naru and Meenau, contain about 90 per cent of the population. More than a third of the islands are not permanently inhabited. Many are not inhabited at all.

Bolivar had brought us, after a five-day journey, to one of these supposedly uninhabited islands. We were moored a short distance off the coast, in the calm, clear water of a tropical lagoon, waiting in beautiful sunshine for Colonel Rory Sisimarama to send out a boat to pick us up.

The island was perhaps six miles across, with many small, hidden bays. It was surprisingly mountainous. The land around the foothills was smothered in palm trees, which sloped down to the water's edge like a thick, tall shag-pile carpet. A carpet with lots of coconuts. And iguanas. And fruit bats. The previous night we had heard them screeching in the trees.

Kiva is renowned as a holiday destination. Tourism is the main industry. People jet in from all over the world to laze around in the lagoons. The island in front of us could easily have been turned into a luxury tourist resort, for the exclusive use of movie stars and other well-heeled patrons. Instead, it had been converted into a secret training base for the ruling Kivanese military and their rugby team. Our new home away from home.

I was up on the bridge of Bolivar's yacht, with Bolivar and Inga and Frank. It was late morning. Bolivar had provided us all with drinks. For the last hour we had been combing over the details of Frank's professional boxing career, which Bolivar knew a lot about. He had seen the fight with the orangutan in Venice. He had seen the fight with the giant panda at Madison Square Garden. He had even seen Frank's very first pro fight as a WWF super-heavyweight, against Herman the Kodiak bear in Chicago. Frank had lost that fight on points, but had come close to knocking Herman out in the early rounds.

'It's a shame you never signed up with me, Frank,' Bolivar said. 'You were good. I could have made you a multi-millionaire.'

'I only work with people I can trust,' Frank said.

'Oh, you could have trusted me,' Bolivar said. 'I am a man of honour. Ask Inga. I *never* go back on my word.'

'Samson believes he is an old-fashioned businessman,' Inga said coolly. 'A deal-maker. An entrepreneur.'

'Yeah, entrepreneur,' I said. 'What a great word that is. How do you spell it again? C-R-O-O-K?'

Bolivar laughed. We had been cooped up together on his yacht for five days, but he had not yet grown tired of our company. We had dined with him. We had watched TV with him. We had played poker with him, for hours at a stretch. I noticed that, if anything, he seemed to enjoy it when I insulted him. Maybe that was because he was normally surrounded by yes-men.

'I could have got you film deals, too,' Bolivar said to Frank. 'Advertising campaigns. Sponsorships. You could have taken it easy for the rest of your life.'

'Don't worry about me, mate,' Frank said. 'I'm doing just fine.'

'What, coaching amateurs at the Institute in Canberra?' Bolivar smiled thinly. 'And looking after a little smart-aleck who can't afford to pay you? I don't think so.'

Out of the corner of my eye, I spotted a glint of grey at the entrance to one of the hidden bays. A Kivanese Navy patrol boat was leaving the island, arcing across the lagoon towards us. Inga saw it, too. Her mouth pursed tight. Once Frank and I left on that patrol boat, it would be much more difficult – if not impossible – for her to help us.

'So tell me,' I said to Bolivar. 'One more thing, before we leave. How did you and the colonel get Hunt off the mainland after you kidnapped him? We all saw the helicopter heading west. And after that – nothing. How'd you get him out here?'

'I didn't kidnap Kelvin Hunt,' Bolivar replied smoothly. 'I had nothing to do with that at all.'

'All right then,' I said. 'How did the *colonel* get Hunt off the mainland? They went up in the chopper, and then what? They disappeared?'

'Why, yes.' Bolivar beamed at me. 'That's exactly what happened. Well done.'

'They must have,' I said. 'Even if you got Hunt out to the coast, say by going overland, on foot, you'd still have to meet up with a boat somewhere offshore. That would be far too risky, with the police swarming everywhere. A boat would be the first thing they'd look for.'

'Precisely,' Bolivar said. 'Although as I say, I am only speculating. I had nothing to do with it at all.'

Shortly afterwards, the Kivanese patrol boat pulled alongside us. We climbed down from the bridge to meet the boarding party. As I turned to descend the ladder, Bolivar was distracted for a moment. Someone called up to him from down below. Quick as a flash, Inga slipped something into my pocket. I had no idea what it was, and I had no time to look. Bolivar turned back towards us, and I continued on as though nothing had happened.

When we were all down on the main deck, a tall, distinguished-looking Kivanese man with long, greying sideburns stepped aboard, flanked by four Kivanese soldiers. The tall man was wearing a dark-blue uniform of shirt and shorts, with socks pulled up neatly to his knees. The four soldiers were dressed in grey.

'Rory,' Bolivar said, as he shook the tall Kivanese by the hand.

'Samson,' the man replied. 'You are late, as usual.'

'It took us a few days to get what you wanted. But he's here.'

Colonel Sisimarama turned to Frank. He did not offer his hand. 'Your friend Mr Hunt speaks very highly of you,' he said. 'He's looking forward to having you on the team. You will do a good job, I'm sure.'

He waited for Frank to respond. Frank didn't say anything. The colonel sized him up coolly for a moment, then turned towards me.

'And this is our new mascot,' he said. 'Let us hope he brings good luck.'

He grinned. The flash of white teeth, contrasting suddenly with his jet-black skin, was startling.

'Actually he brings bad luck,' Bolivar said. 'He's a pest. You'll have to watch him.'

'Oh, I think both our guests will be watched very closely,' the colonel said. 'They will be well behaved. They are a long way from home. Nobody knows where they are. And the penalty for bad behaviour is . . . extremely severe.'

18. Welcome To My Nightmare

The four soldiers marshalled us aboard the patrol boat. We were locked in a room the size of a broom cupboard for the trip back to shore. On our arrival, we were handcuffed and blindfolded and bundled into the back of a jeep. Two soldiers squeezed in beside us in the back. The other two sat with the driver in the front, with guns at the ready.

'This wasn't in the brochure,' I said to Frank as we bumped and jolted our way inland along a winding, dusty road.

The colonel was no longer with us. He had taken a separate jeep on a separate road. We were being looked after by our armed guard of four, who either didn't speak

English or didn't want to speak to us. Nobody said a word for nearly ten minutes, as we weaved through the palm trees, up and over a series of low foothills, further and further inland.

Our destination was quite spectacular. Our guards were kind enough to remove our blindfolds as soon as the jeep pulled up. We had reached a clearing in the jungle, into which had been built a sprawling, state-of-the-art, multi-sport training facility. Back when I'd played junior rep football, before the car accident that shattered my knee, I'd attended some training sessions at the Glendale Centre in Newcastle. That was what this place reminded me of. It had a brand-spanking-new 400-metre running track, with a perfectly groomed sports field in the middle. Facilities for high jump, long jump, javelin, discus, hammer. Portable football goals, as well as rugby posts and scrum machines.

A three-storey building to our left was

obviously the headquarters. A gymnasium and some dormitories were located behind that. Another two rugby pitches stretched away to our right, as well as a hockey pitch, a second football pitch and an indoor swimming pool. There were changing rooms. Floodlights. A massage and sauna centre. The 100-metre track marked out directly in front of us was littered with the same sort of specialist equipment I'd seen at the Institute, to measure flexibility and speed.

We stood for a few moments, taking it all in, before the soldiers pushed and prodded us toward the dorms.

'So this is the secret weapon of the new Kivanese government,' I said to Frank. 'Part of their master plan to take over the world.'

Kelvin Hunt came out from the headquarters to meet us. Two more soldiers – or naval officers, or Kivanese killbots, whatever they were – came out with him. Hunt looked a fair bit thinner than last time we'd seen him, and quite a lot more sunburned. But otherwise he looked OK.

'Frankie-boy,' he said, shooting Frank a nervous grin as our minders took off the handcuffs. 'Good to see you. Welcome to my nightmare.'

He held out his hand. Frank shook it only reluctantly.

'Why me, Kel?' Frank said.

'I had no choice.' Hunt gave a jittery laugh. 'There were some other blokes I could've picked, but they all had wives and kids. You didn't. In the end it came down to that.'

'And what about Fletcher?'

'I had no idea they'd bring him. I'm sorry.'

We headed back towards the dormitories. All six soldiers followed us without a word. Apparently we got two each, to help us stay out of trouble.

'You'll get used to them, boys,' Hunt told us. 'They'll shadow you everywhere.'

A moment later he went on. 'So tell me.

What's going on back home? My wife –?'

'She's good,' Frank said. 'Your whole family's holding up. We've seen them on TV. They're doing fine.'

'They won't let me send anything. No mail. No message. Nothing. We're completely cut off here.'

'Until the next World Cup?' I said. 'Is that the plan?'

Hunt stopped walking. We had reached one of several entrances to the dormitories. They were just like the dormitories back at the Institute, only strangely empty of people. 'I've got no idea what the plan is,' he said. 'This place is not just about rugby, as you can see. They've got athletics here. Swimming. Hockey. Gymnastics. You name it. The colonel is convinced that if he can turn out world-class sporting teams, the Kivanese people will accept his one-party rule. They'll be so busy cheering on their teams, they won't notice they're living in a police state.'

'Sounds like a smart plan to me,' Frank said. 'It's a wonder nobody thought of it back home.'

'You'd never get away with this back home,' Hunt said. 'Somebody would talk. Some nosy journalist would blow the lid on the whole caper. Here, nobody talks. There's no free media. No journalists except the ones employed by the army. The army runs everything in this joint. Including us, as you can see.'

He gestured to the six soldiers accompanying us. He didn't seem afraid to talk openly in front of them. I guess he wasn't saying anything they didn't know already.

'I'm supposed to be in charge of the athletics programme as well as the rugby teams,' he went on. 'Can you believe that? The colonel thinks that because I can do speed training for rugby players, I can train Olympic sprinters and middle-distance runners. He's a dreamer, he's got a grand vision, but he's not good on practical detail. The training schedules in this place are an absolute shambles.'

Our six minders showed us to our rooms. As Hunt had predicted, they followed us everywhere. I inspected the toilet block at the end of the hall, hoping to finally get time to look at what Inga had slipped into my pocket. My two minders – who I began to think of as B1 and B2 – came in with me. They wouldn't even let me go to the toilet on my own.

The place wasn't crowded. But it *felt* crowded with so many soldiers around. Hunt told us to try to pretend they weren't there. The three of us sat around in Frank's room for a while, not quite knowing what to say. Then Hunt started talking about the athletes' conditioning programmes, and how Frank would fit in.

'Mostly, the athletes train for two hours in the morning, then have a break and do some sports psychology,' he said. 'That's where they are now, the whole lot of them. They're upstairs in the main building, watching a video.'

'Sports psych with the Kivanese military, eh?' I said. 'How's that go? Win every game, or we kill you?'

'Something like that, yeah.' Hunt managed a weak smile. 'Anyway, there's another afternoon session for two hours. And now you're here, the colonel wants to add another session in the evening, just for speed and conditioning.'

'Three sessions a day?' Frank frowned. 'In this heat?'

'No choice, mate,' Hunt shrugged. 'That's what he wants. He's read somewhere that three sessions a day is optimum. So that's it. No arguments. What the colonel wants, the colonel gets, my friend. Every time.'

19. TINFOIL

The six soldiers standing by the door gave no sign they had understood. Maybe they had, maybe they hadn't. Personally, I wouldn't have risked criticising the colonel at all. Not even mildly. But the Kelvinator was used to speaking his mind.

'Are they any good, these athletes?' I asked. 'What are your rugby players like?'

'With me coaching, they could be competitive,' Hunt admitted, with characteristic modesty. 'Their set pieces are improving every day. Their defence is tight. Their line-outs are organised. They're winning their practice games. We had a game against Japan last week, which I'm sure you didn't read about. Won it by 15 points.'

'And you stay here and watch on video?'
I said.

'I'm on video link-up with 'em all the time,' Hunt said. 'But it's not the same, kid. It's tough giving a half-time team talk on video. What if I want to throw a chair at someone? Or clout someone round the ear? I'm 6,000 miles away.'

'So was the colonel happy when you beat Japan?' Frank asked.

'He won't be happy till we beat the All Blacks,' Hunt said. 'Or the Springboks. Or the Wallabies. And that might take a while.'

We spent the rest of the day cooped up in the dorms. Frank got busy catching up with paperwork, in preparation for his new job. He had mountains of print-outs to go through. His first session with the Kivanese rugby team was at five o'clock that same evening. I wasn't allowed to attend, but fortunately the session was outdoors, on the running track with all the measuring equipment, which was visible from my bedroom window. I actually ended up with a pretty good view.

Frank made them do a speed session, using the resistance equipment. Lead weights, parachutes, tyres, that kind of thing. Speed has always been the Kivanese's strong point, and most of those boys could really move. I doubt there was a player on the squad coming in over eleven seconds for the hundred. And that included the forwards. Even with lead weights strapped to their wrists and ankles, tyres dragging on ropes behind them, and parachutes flying out behind, they tore up the track like demons. It was almost worth being kidnapped, just to watch them go.

There were other athletes going through their paces as well. Hockey players playing under floodlights. Swimmers making their way to and from the pool. It was quite an entertaining spectacle. My two minders – B1 and B2 – watched it from the other window. That gave me the chance to check my pocket, to see what Inga had slipped in there, back on the top deck of Bolivar's yacht.

It was some tinfoil.

Inga had given me a tray of tiny white pills.

I managed a quick glance down at them. There was no brand name on the tinfoil. No information on what they were for. They could have been pills to change me into a cocker spaniel, for all I knew.

At dinner time some of the soldiers finished their shift. Hunt and Frank and I ate in the dining room, down the other end of the room from the soldiers and athletes. All the athletes were on a western diet, not a traditional Kivanese one. Lots of bread, red meat, salads and vegetables. Then for dessert they had pancakes – just like the Wallabies at Coffs Harbour. A ten-stack of pancakes with maple syrup. The international athlete's best friend.

After dinner, before they left for the dorms, Hunt's rugby players did something very surprising. They brought all their chairs in close together around one table and sang hymns. They sang three songs in their native language, all perfectly in tune. I'd spent a lot of time with sports teams over the last few years, in camp or at the Institute, but I'd never seen a team sing hymns before. It was great.

By the time they sang their last song, I was almost asleep. It had been an exhausting, whirlwind seven days, from the moment Frank and I had first left Canberra for our meeting with Holden McGroyne. I hadn't slept well on Bolivar's yacht. Boats in general don't agree with me, not even big luxury cruisers with air-conditioning, flatscreen TV, and a mini bar. I was so tired I had to force my eyes open to keep myself from nodding off.

I was sitting there trying to fight off sleep when it hit me. The capsules Inga had slipped into my pocket. *They were sleeping pills.* Or rather, they were *knockout* pills –

benzodiazepines. Similar to Rohypnol. And they weren't meant for me at all. They were meant for my guards.

Benzodiazepines are illegal in Australia, but Inga had once mentioned to me that she had some. If Bolivar ever found out what she was doing, she told me, the pills might give her one last chance to escape. Attack is the best form of defence, she said. Once her cover was blown, she wasn't going to wait around and be killed. Two pills in Bolivar's drink, and it would be good night, Irene.

The pills were designed to dissolve in seconds. They took between five and ten minutes to work. I had to find a way to slip a couple to B1 and B2.

Little glasses filled with toothpicks had been placed on every table in the dining room. The Kivanese, I noticed, liked to clean their teeth with these after their meal. I picked up a glassful of toothpicks as the rugby team finished singing, just to muck around with them. A few seconds later,

I began to get the faint inklings of a plan.

'Could you lend me some money?' I asked Hunt as we got up to leave. 'Just some loose change, maybe some dollar coins?'

'Kid, you don't need money here,' Hunt said. 'There's nothing to buy. And if you think you can bribe the guards, forget it. You can't.'

'It's not for bribing the guards,' I said. 'I've got another plan. Anything you've got would be good.'

Puzzled, Hunt dug in his pocket. He came out clutching three one-dollar coins, a couple of two-dollars, and a 50-cent coin. 'That enough?' he said.

'Plenty,' I said. 'Once I'm free, I'll come and get you. Be ready.'

Hunt laughed. 'Sure, kid. But I think you've been watching too many movies.'

I took a handful of toothpicks from the glass I'd been holding and put them in my pocket. The soldiers had seen all this, of course. They couldn't hear what we were saying, but they'd seen what was going on. As I went to walk out the door, they stopped me, and one of them pointed to my pocket. I wasn't sure if they understood English or not. None of the soldiers guarding us ever said a word.

'It's for a game,' I explained to them. 'Later. Back in my room. We need these, some money and a glass of water. Come on, I'll show you how to play.'

20. Something in The Water

Men are strange creatures. Most of them are, anyway. Show them two flies crawling up a window and they'll declare it a race and try to pick a winner. They'll give their fly a name. They'll deck it out with colours. They'll place bets on it, and discuss its form in the eight days since it's been born and the condition of the glass it's crawling on. Then they'll argue for hours that it should've got to the top first, when it didn't.

The game I had in mind was very simple. Two people try to throw toothpicks into a glass of water, from a set distance. The distance can be two metres, three, five. Whatever you think you can handle. You bet a small amount of money on each round, with the first player to land a toothpick in the glass declared the winner.

The winner gets the money. The loser has to drink the glass.

Back at my room in the dormitory, I filled up a glass of water and set it down in the middle of the floor. I paced out three metres, then chose myself a decent-looking supersonic Mach-4 toothpick. Before I threw it, I took out my 50-cent piece and laid it on the table for everyone to see.

'It's yours, if you beat me,' I said to B1 and B2, who were watching curiously from near the door. 'Don't spend it all at once.'

I threw the toothpick and missed the glass. It's a lot harder than it looks to get a toothpick to fly straight for three metres. Try it sometime. You'll see what I mean. I was more used to playing this game with matches, too, which are shorter and heavier at the nose, thus giving them a more predictable and accurate glass-finding trajectory.

'Roll up, gents,' I said. 'Hit the glass at three metres, and win the money. Roll up, roll up. Everyone's a winner here. You can't lose.'

I picked up the toothpick, returned to my mark, and threw again. I missed by even more this time. By now the two soldiers were smiling. One of them applauded as my toothpick spiralled way off-course and landed on the floor. They nudged each other, talking together in their own language. The one who had applauded put down his rifle and stepped forward.

'I will play,' he said.

'Right you are, champ,' I replied, and shook his hand. 'Toothpicks at three metres. The Kivanese death machine versus the cute little white boy. Choose your weapon.'

B1 chose a toothpick. We lined up for the first round. After nearly a dozen shots, the soldier finally landed his toothpick in the glass. Did he celebrate? You bet he did. You would've thought he'd just sunk an eagle on the 18th to win the Kivanese Open. He roared in triumph, threw his hands in the air, and danced all around the room.

I drank the water, parted with my 50 cents, and took out a gold coin. Now we were into the serious money. Before we started the gold-coin round, I had to refill the glass. There was a small kitchenette in the corner of the room, with a sink and a tap. Standing at the sink with my back to the soldiers, I quickly dropped in two of Inga's knockout pills.

I shielded the glass behind my fingers as the pills dissolved. By the time I laid it down on the floor again, everything looked normal. The benzodiazepine was odourless, colourless and tasteless. Nobody could tell the difference between drugged water and plain. I just needed to make sure that it wasn't me that drank it. I *had* to win the next round.

I hadn't been trying before. I did now. Still, my first shot was a near-miss. B1 stepped up and almost landed his. It caught the rim of the glass and spun off to the side. My second shot needed to be good, and it was: a magnificent toothpick swan-dive, sailing through the air and landing point-first in the middle of the water. Ten out of ten.

The soldier drained the glass. I took it from him and returned to the sink. Two more pills went secretly into the water, exactly as before. I had five minutes until my first victim keeled over unconscious.

'What about you, mate?' I said, pointing to B2 standing by the door. 'Don't you want to play?'

B2 nodded. My gold coin was still on the table. He placed a Kivanese coin beside it, then picked out a toothpick of his own. With B1 standing guard, he took his first shot, and missed wildly. I then missed as well. My toothpick was wet – it clung to the tips of my fingers just as I threw it. I threw the wet toothpick away, rubbed my fingers against my shorts to dry them, then took a fresh one.

B2 missed a second time. I stepped up to the mark, got myself into the zone, and fired. Another direct hit. Another perfect ten. If there was a scholarship to the Institute of Sport for toothpick throwing, I would have it in the bag. Unfortunately, there's not a lot of money in toothpick throwing at the moment. Sponsors are hard to come by. The international professional circuit is rather small.

I waited till B2 had drained his glass, then announced that I needed to go to the toilet. A quick glance at my watch told me that three and a half minutes had passed since B1 had downed his glass. I took my time walking down the hall, and even more time doing what I had to do in the little boys' room. B2 accompanied me this time. B1 stayed back at the ranch. I needed to keep B2 occupied in the toilet for another four minutes, until the drug kicked in. I couldn't let him walk back into my dorm room and see his partner on the floor, out cold.

I faked a bit of constipation. I won't go into the details. Four minutes later I was still there, clutching my stomach and doing a good impersonation of a cow giving birth to triplets. B2 was starting to get a trifle annoyed.

'Sorry,' I told him. 'I'm not feeling well. Must be something in the water.'

B2 blinked at me slowly. For a moment he looked like he'd forgotten something. He raised a hand to rub his forehead, then kept it there, as if glued to his skin. He began swaying in the doorway, then checked himself against the doorframe to stop himself from falling over.

'Whatever it is, looks like you've got it too,' I said.

His knees buckled. He slumped to the floor. On my way out, I checked his pulse. It was even. He was breathing nice and slow. I relieved him of his semi-automatic, then hurried back to check the situation in my dorm room. The situation was excellent. Tweedledum was out for the count as well. Two down, four to go. I turned and ran.

21. Break-out!

It was pitch-dark outside, which was just as well, considering I was the only white kid in the neighbourhood. In daylight, I stuck out like a sore thumb. I ran to the next dormitory block, in the side entrance, and up the stairs to Frank's room. I burst in without knocking, trying to look like I knew how to use the semi-automatic, and ordered Frank's two minders up against the wall.

Frank took their guns off them and made them sit on the floor. He tore up the top bedsheet and tied them to the bedposts. He tore up the bottom bedsheet to make gags. We proceeded to the next dormitory block and into Hunt's room, where Frank did the business on Hunt's two minders. Six down, none to go.

We escaped on foot. Despite the gags, the four soldiers who were still conscious started making a hell of a noise. We really should have knocked them out, but Frank was too much of a softie. One day they're going to have to write that on his grave.

Hunt and Frank agreed that the best thing would be to follow the road away from the training base, back to the lagoon. Maybe we could find a radio room somewhere, and get off a call for help. Maybe we could hijack a patrol boat. We didn't need to make it all the way back to Australia – just to the Australian High Commission on Meenau. Or anywhere public enough that Bolivar and Colonel Sisimarama would think twice about gunning us down.

We paused for breath after ten minutes running, hiding in some bushes by the side of the road. There was no sign of traffic travelling to and from the base. It wouldn't be long, however. Thanks to our minders, the alarm would soon be raised, and the whole island would be swarming with troops.

'All right, kid,' Hunt said, after he had gulped down a dozen large mouthfuls of air, and got most of his breath back. 'Come clean. How'd you get past those two guards?'

'Toothpicks,' I said.

'Toothpicks,' Hunt repeated. 'Uh huh. What'd you do, dip 'em in poison?'

'No, in water,' I said. Then, when he frowned, I added, 'It's an ancient Navajo Indian trick. I'll show you sometime.'

We kept near the road, always keeping an ear open for traffic. It was hard to hear anything at all above the sound of the fruit bats. After a while, the noise of their screeching grew so loud that I stopped worrying about soldiers, and started worrying about fruit bats. They were supposed to be harmless, but they sounded demented. How big were fruit bats, anyway? What if they got sick of eating fruit? If they did have a taste for human flesh, I could only hope they'd go for Frank and Kelvin Hunt first. Both of them had a lot more meat on their bones.

We reached the lagoon at 3.30 in the morning. Only then did we realise that somehow we'd taken the wrong road. It wasn't the same quiet, peaceful lagoon we'd landed at the previous day. This lagoon was much larger. The jetty extending out into it was much larger as well. In fact, there were several jetties – an entire naval base – spread right around the bay. A frigate, six patrol boats and a whole flotilla of civilian launches were tied up there. A depot just back from the shore housed two rows of army trucks, and maybe 20 jeeps, all enclosed in barbed wire. Beyond that was a helicopter compound, complete with helipad, pilots' headquarters and two choppers.

We had an excellent view of everything, because all the lights around the base were blazing. Soldiers were running everywhere. Jeeps and trucks were driving off into the night. Either Kiva was being invaded by Fiji, or they were looking for us. I didn't have to think too hard to guess which.

We stayed under cover, taking in the scene. It got busier and busier. Our chances of hijacking a patrol boat or sneaking into a radio room were precisely nil. After a while, my gaze fell on the helicopters, one of which looked strangely familiar to me. A few seconds later, I recognised it. It was a Panther. A helicopter exactly like it had been used to kidnap Kelvin Hunt.

I pointed this out to Frank. He nodded. The colour, the shape, the lack of markings: everything was the same. Hunt wasn't so sure. He'd been knocked out too early in the piece to get a good view of it, and had been drugged for the rest of the trip. But Frank and I had no doubt at all.

'Which means,' I said, 'Maybe Bolivar was right. Maybe they did escape by chopper.'

'They could have refuelled on the frigate,' Frank suggested. 'Take a look. It's got a helipad, too.'

'But how did they get off the mainland?' I said. 'We heard them go west. Everybody did.'

Frank shrugged. 'Beats me.'

'And another thing,' I said. 'Why did the Kivanese need to buy weapons from Cameron Maddox? They've got weapons of their own, surely.'

'Too easily traced,' Frank said. 'Much better to use black-market equipment. It could belong to anybody.'

Just then two men emerged from the pilots' HQ and boarded the Panther. A few minutes later, the rotors began spinning. The engine noise built up to a crescendo. The chopper lifted slowly into the night sky.

'You see?' I shouted at Frank. 'There's no way they could have escaped in that. You can't hide something that loud!'

A minute later, however, something

extraordinary happened. We were watching the helicopter hover over the bay, with the noise of the rotors still pounding in our ears, when all of a sudden the noise cut out. It died completely. The helicopter went whisper-quiet. It was still flying. The rotors were still turning. *But they were making absolutely no noise.* As we watched, dumbfounded, the lights went off inside the cabin. The helicopter banked to the left and headed, silent and invisible, out over the lagoon.

22. THE OUTRIGGER

Half an hour later, we spotted the outrigger. It was pulled up on the beach beside the jetty at the southernmost end of the bay. We had slowly worked our way around to the south, keeping under cover of the palm trees, trying to figure out a way to get off the island. So far, we had no bright ideas.

The problem with all the military hardware was that there were far too many military personnel looking after it. And time was running out. Soon they would figure out that we might be at the lagoon, and start systematically searching the jungle. I guessed we had 15 minutes to make up our minds.

The outrigger was a traditional wooden

fishing boat about 18 feet long, with a canvas sail and two sturdy wooden paddles stowed neatly inside the hull. Several fishing lines and some buckets filled with other fishing gear were also stowed in there. So were some ropes, a jag-hook, and a 20-litre plastic water container, half full.

'This could get us to the next island,' Frank said. 'No worries.'

'Great,' I said. 'So where is the next island?'

'I don't know,' Frank admitted. 'But there are more than 200 of them. We're bound to hit one.'

Hunt stared at the outrigger incredulously. 'You're kidding!' he said. 'Look around! A hundred million dollars worth of naval equipment, and you want to take the hollowed-out log?'

'People survive for weeks in boats like these,' Frank said.

'Yeah,' Hunt quipped. 'But not with the Kivanese Navy trying to sink them.

And usually those people know how to sail.'

'I don't think we've got a choice, Kel,' Frank said. 'It's this or nothing. We've got to go.'

My main worry was that we would be spotted before we got out of the bay. The closest jetty was only 100 metres away. It appeared to be deserted, but appearances could be deceptive. If one eagle-eyed Kivanese soldier spotted us trying to sneak around the headland, we were done for.

We dragged the boat into the water and got in. Frank took the tiller while Hunt and I fiddled with the sail. Dawn had broken, but it was still quite dark. The boat would be hard to spot, silhouetted against the jungle. The breeze was up. We were making good speed towards the open sea. We had a good chance. A fighting chance. We would've made it, if it hadn't been for the chopper. The mission it had left on earlier had been abandoned. Unknown to us, it had come back to base to help with the search. The first we knew about that was when a powerful searchlight switched on, high above us, illuminating the outrigger and the lagoon all around.

'Uh oh,' Frank said.

'Give me a rifle,' Hunt growled. 'I'll blow it out of the sky.'

'Head back to land!' I said. 'We can lose them in the jungle!'

'There's another boat,' Frank said. 'It's coming out to get us.'

I could see the lights of a small civilian craft speeding towards us from the naval base. Frank held course towards the open sea. Hunt did his best to help by taking some pot-shots at the helicopter. He then turned his aim on the speedboat, which was racing closer and closer, only 300 metres away now.

'Cut it out!' Frank roared. 'We're sitting ducks here!'

'You want me?' Hunt yelled. 'Come and get me, you turkeys!'

The lagoon erupted around us. The

surface of the water became a trampoline, bouncing us up. The boat, Hunt, Frank, myself – everything lifted and tumbled. Water swirled like wind. Wind swirled like water. I went down into a trough, came up into a wave, went under again. The second time I got to the surface, everything was still.

The missile had gone off just ahead of us. A warning shot. The outrigger was floating on its side, capsized. I was in the water close to the sail. Frank and Hunt were on the other side. The speedboat was already pulling alongside Hunt. Soldiers were reaching down, preparing to haul him aboard. Colonel Rory Sisimarama was standing impassively in the stern.

'Fascists!' Hunt yelled, flailing about as the soldiers grabbed him. 'Mongrels! Philistines!'

He was hauled aboard, dripping and swearing. Frank and I, meanwhile, had returned to the capsized canoe. We waited there, clinging to the upturned hull, as the speedboat closed in.

Colonel Sisimarama moved to the side of the boat nearer us. 'Fletcher Smith,' he said contemptuously. 'Samson told me you would bring us bad luck. I didn't believe him. Unfortunately, it was true.'

He motioned for two soldiers to join him at the side of the boat.

'I am a very superstitious man,' the colonel continued. 'I don't like black cats. I never walk under ladders. When I find something that is causing me bad luck, I eliminate it.'

He turned to the two soldiers standing beside him. 'We will take no more chances,' he said. 'Kill them.'

The soldiers raised their weapons. I shut my eyes. Perhaps I should have done more to save myself, or at least tried to. I could have dived underwater. I could have tried to hide under the sail. But somehow it seemed too late for that. The bullets would come too quickly.

I shut my eyes tighter, hugged the upturned hull of the outrigger, and waited. Nothing happened.

Still nothing happened.

I opened my eyes to see that the soldiers had lowered their weapons. They and the colonel were staring past the outrigger towards the open sea. I turned and saw another boat nosing its way around the point of the headland. A boat the size of a patrol boat, but with different markings. Its lights were different. It rode differently in the water. Was it a fishing boat? A coast-guard vessel? In the half-light of the Kivanese dawn, it was difficult to tell.

The colonel seemed frozen to the spot. Obviously the arrival of this boat was completely unexpected. One of the soldiers murmured something to him. He nodded curtly. Above us, the helicopter switched off its searchlight and headed silently back to land.

'Ha!' Hunt wrestled free of his captors,

grinning deliriously. 'Now you're in for it, you maggots! It's the Australian Navy! *They'll* sort you out!'

But it wasn't the Australian Navy. As it drew closer, I made out the words 'Coast Guard' painted on the side of the hull. Did that mean it was the Kivanese coast guard? If so, wasn't that under the control of the colonel, too? Why had he backed off when more of his own men were approaching? What did it matter if they saw us gunned down as well?

It wasn't until the boat pulled alongside us that I understood.

Detective Inspector Flintoff and Lieutenant Calabria were standing at the stern.

23. Debriefing

We didn't get the full story until an hour later. By that time we were sitting in the cabin of the coast-guard boat in dry clothes, heading back to Kiva Naru before flying home. The island of Colonel Sisimarama had almost disappeared below the horizon behind us. So had the mad colonel himself. A woman from the Australian High Commission in Meenau was with us. She'd taken Hunt to the ship's radio so he could talk to his wife and kids. Lieutenant Calabria was calmly sipping a cup of coffee beside me, looking like she made raids on secret Kivanese naval bases every morning of her life.

'I hate rescuing you, Smith,' Flintoff

growled, as he puffed and wheezed his way into the room. 'It feels all wrong. It goes right against the grain.'

'Well, maybe you should try solving your own cases in future,' I said.

Flintoff's face went heart-attack purple again. His favourite colour.

'We did solve it!' he barked. 'That's why we're here! And we could have done without you and your ugly pet Turk running off half-cocked, getting yourselves into trouble that we had to get you out of!'

'Was it the footprint?' I said to Lieutenant Calabria, ignoring Flintoff and his blustering. 'Is that what tipped you off?'

The lieutenant nodded, setting down her coffee. 'It's a submariner's print,' she said. 'Standard-issue boot from the Kivanese Navy. Took me a while to match it, but I got there in the end.'

'OK,' I said. 'So they transferred Hunt to a sub once they got out into international waters? Is that right?'

'Yes. Then the chopper went back to the frigate. And the sub took Hunt and the kidnappers back here. Very clever.'

'But how did you know which island we were on?' Frank asked.

'We got a tip-off,' Lieutenant Calabria said. 'A phone call. Untraceable. Someone gave us the latitude and longitude of the island, then hung up.'

'Inga,' I murmured.

Flintoff glared at me. 'Who?' he demanded. 'What? What did you say?'

'Nothing,' I said.

'So what happens to Sisimarama now?' Frank said. 'Can you arrest him?'

'No. He's a head of government,' Lieutenant Calabria shrugged. 'We can issue a strongly worded diplomatic protest, maybe. You know the type. *"The Australian Government expresses its grave disapproval at this blatant breach of its sovereignty, etc, etc."* The media will have a field day, of course. But Sisimarama won't care.'

'He cares about sport,' I said. 'What about sanctions? Can't we get him banned from international competition?'

'That just punishes the rest of the country,' Lieutenant Calabria said. 'And the players as well. It's not their fault he's making them do this. The people of his country are suffering enough.'

'You could arrest Bolivar, though,' Frank said.

Lieutenant Calabria looked puzzled. 'Why should we do that?' she said.

'He was in on this from the beginning,' I explained. 'He's the one who brought us to Kiva. On his yacht.'

'You didn't come with the Kivanese?' Lieutenant Calabria asked.

'No. Cameron Maddox delivered us to Bolivar's yacht in Sydney. We were on it with him for five days.'

Flintoff had been listening in stony silence. Now he leant forward, placing both hands knuckle-first on the table in front of us.

'That's a very serious allegation you're making, Smith,' he said. 'Got any *proof*?'

'Yes,' I said. 'Ask the colonel. He'll confirm Frank and I weren't on any of his boats. And besides, Bolivar's still got my wallet and mobile phone. If you search his yacht, you'll find them. Get a search warrant, and –'

'I thought so.' Flintoff stood up again, grinning triumphantly. 'Nothing. You're clutching at straws, kid. You just can't resist it, can you? Well, let me tell you something. If you mention Bolivar's name again, I will *personally* ring the Kivanese government and give you back to them. Free of charge.'

We separated at the airport. Flintoff was staying in Kiva to deal with the media. Lieutenant Calabria was flying back to Brisbane with Hunt. Frank and I were headed for Sydney, en route to Canberra, but we had to wait around for another few hours before catching our flight. The lady from the Australian High Commission in

Meenau was going to stay with us, just to be on the safe side.

Hunt was going straight into camp with the Wallabies. They had a game against South Africa the following weekend. Frank was going to have a week's break, then join them. I was invited along, but I still felt a bit low about not catching Bolivar. Right then I hadn't made up my mind.

'You know the best thing?' Hunt grinned at us. 'I get to sack Lachlan Maddox all over again.'

'And I get to arrest him,' Lieutenant Calabria said. 'Along with his brother. For murder.'

'You boys did a top job back there,' Hunt told us, shaking our hands vehemently as the flight to Brisbane was called. 'Toothpicks, eh?' he winked at me. 'You'll have to show me that trick sometime.'

'By the way, Frank,' Lieutenant Calabria said, just before she turned to go. 'I forgot to tell you. Your car's been stolen.'

'Oh no!' Frank buried his head in his hands. 'Not the Corvette! I've only had it six months!'

'The Sydney police are looking for it. It'll probably turn up somewhere. Joyriders, y'know –'

'They'll torch it,' Frank moaned. 'Do you know how much the insurance excess is on that thing? I'll have to pay thousands!'

'That shouldn't be a problem.' Lieutenant Calabria grinned. 'The reward will more than cover it.'

'Reward?' Frank and I said, both at the same time.

'Sure. The reward. A hundred thousand dollars, for information leading to Hunt's release or recapture. Didn't you read about that?'

'No,' I said. 'Bolivar didn't give us any newspapers. Neither did the colonel. We'll have to write to the Kivanese Tourist Board about that.'

'Well, it's there waiting to be collected,'

the lieutenant said. 'And I'll make sure you get it. You deserve every cent.'

Hunt and Lieutenant Calabria joined the queue to board the plane. Hearing about the reward money made me feel a whole lot better. Bolivar might have got away again, but one day his luck would run out. One day very soon.

I was hungry. I looked across the terminal to the food court. Even the salad bar looked good.

'My shout, Frankie,' I said. 'I'll buy you a sandwich.'

'Hey – you owe me, kid,' Frank said. 'Make it two.'

About The Author

Jonathan Harlen wrote his first novel when he was eight years old. Unfortunately, he spelt his own name wrong on the front cover. Since then he has had over 20 novels published, for children and adults. He lives with his family on a small farm on the far north coast of New South Wales. Jonathan has worked as a journalist, radio comedian, landscape gardener and rock musician, but he dreams of one day being an A-League football coach.

Jonathan has always wanted to write a series set in the world of elite professional sport, which is full of drama and skulduggery. In 2006, he spent five days working with the football coaches at the Australian Institute of Sport in Canberra. While he was there the idea of a sports detective based at the AIS came to him out of the blue. It nestled in his brain and eventually Fletcher Smith was born.